CLASSIC PULP FICTION

Death Walks in the Fog | Charles Boeckman 3
Seelingson's number was nearly up, but he could choose his death.

Face to Infinity | E. C. Tubb 13
Here one minute ... flashback or flash forward the next ...

Bloody Bill Obeys | Erle Stanley Gardner 41
The stage magician needed a volunteer, but he chose Bloody Bill.

Werewoman | C. L. Moore 87
An ancient evil bayed at the moon, but Northwest Smith had business.

The Tree-Man | Henry S. Whitehead 105
Pineapples, coconuts, hatred ...

Killer's Choice | Earle Basinsky 127
On a foggy night, "Rocky" placed Captain Alan in a bad spot.

NEW PULP FICTION

Let's Not Argue | Conrad Adamson 9
A shopping list didn't include danger or love ...

Case Gray | Robert J. Mendenhall 21
War ... and zombies! An "unusual" case for Code Name: Intrepid.

Mona's Back | Michael A. Wexler 49
She walked right out of his life, and right back into a mob war!

Welcoming Amethyst Eyes | Steven L. Rowe 69
When a duel is imminent, it helps for the eyes to drink in the prize.

PULP HISTORY

A Tale of Two Stories | David Goudsward 75
C. L. Moore "Werewoman"; Henry S. Whitehead "The Tree-Man"

The Case for Erle Stanley Gardner | Michael Brown 39
Remembering the creator of Perry Mason, crusading attorney ...

DEPARTMENTS

Editorial | Audrey Parente 2

Rich Harvey | Publisher
Audrey Parente | Editor

Additional thanks:
Morgan Wallace,
Michael Brown
Philip Harbottle
David Goudsward

Cover by Howell Dodd
Best True Fact Detective
January 1950

ISBN-13: 9798668261703

Pulp Adventures TM & © 2020 Bold Venture Press. All Rights Reserved. Published quarterly. Any similarities to actual persons living or dead (in the fiction) is purely coincidental.

Most story submissions for *Pulp Adventures* blip into Bold Venture Press electronically. Occasionally our postman squashes paper manuscripts into Box #105 in the loggia of our building.

Regardless of how the works arrive, reading each story is a sort of challenge, even a dare, to find something evocative, a knockout punch-in-the-gut piece of work to match the classic pulp styles we reprint. We search for writers who have the right pen stroke to entertain a discerning crowd already addicted to pulp fiction. Not everyone is a good writer, even if there's a good story behind the pen.

What a treat when the story is superb and the writer top notch. All this is part of the mission for *Pulp Adventures*. Another part of the package, which we will be trying to do more often, is to bring some background to the stories we reprint — essays by pulp collectors and interested historians.

This issue features *two* scholarly articles. First, Pulp Super-fan Michael Brown makes the case for attorney-turned-author Erle Stanley Gardner. His article accompanies a never-before reprinted tale, "Bloody Bill Obeys," from a 1924 issue of the weekly *Chicago Ledger* story paper.

Morgan Wallace discovered Gardner's lost tale several years ago. He awaited the proper opportunity to return it to print, and we're glad he decided *Pulp Adventures* was the best showcase for Perry Mason's raconteur.

Next on the docket, David Goudsward follows the revisionist history of two classic stories. Henry S. Whitehead and C.L. Moore were celebrated contributors to *Weird Tales*. Though "Werewoman" and "The Tree-Man" are cornerstones of their careers, the authors apparently remained unsatisfied with the results, and revised their stories … and remained unsatisfied … and revised yet again …

Our previous issue (#35) marked the *Pulp Adventures* debut of illustrator Howard Simpson, illustrating "Give 'Em Hell, Helen" by Adam McFarlane. Despite his formidable talent, Howard graciously found the time to illustrate Adam's story — and what an illustration! Pen and ink are Howard's tools. Very rare to find an illustrator these days who does not rely on computer graphics, and the result serves as its own testimony.

Clayton Hinkle debuts in this issue, illustrating "Welcoming Amethyst Eyes" by Steven L. Rowe. Clayton painted the cover for John E. Petty's *Outlaw: The Legend of Robin Hood Book One*. Welcome aboard, Clayton!

Enjoy this issue!

— *Audrey Parente*

Seelingson's number was nearly up, but he could still choose his manner of death — and his vengeance!

Death Walks In the Fog

BY CHARLES BOECKMAN, JR.

JOHN SEELINGSON couldn't see the man who was following him; fog, dense like rain immobilized in the atmosphere, concealed him. The man had a gun, and Seelingson knew that before the night passed the gun was going to kill him.

He was walking toward a settlement-house where the man who stole his wife — Doctor Michael Evans — operated a free part-time clinic. The fog-enshrouded lights of the building came into view; he moved up the worn steps and through the door. Behind him, the form of the hired killer paused and drew back into the gray mist.

The girl behind the desk reminded Seelingson of the many he'd seen like her in criminal court, where he had practiced for years; pretty, but shopworn. The cynical hardness around her mouth had softened somewhat though, as if she'd recently been treated nice for the first time in her life.

In answer to his inquiry about Doctor Evans, she said that he'd treated some patients at the clinic tonight and left a few minutes before. "I hope nothing is wrong," she said, looking into Seelingson's middle-aged face.

"No," he replied.

"Are you a patient of his?" she asked.

"A friend," he lied, wanting information.

His words released a spring of hidden beauty within her and it flowed into her face. "I think I know where he is," she said. "He went to call on one of the boys who is sick."

She turned to a filing cabinet and found a card. "Here it is." She gave Seelingson a number. He thanked her and went out.

The address she had given him was deep in the heart of the slum district. Here, the tenement houses lurked unpainted and squalid in the darkness. He moved along the sidewalk, a bulky, silent figure, wrapped in gloom; behind him the footsteps of the hired killer beat through the fog.

Tap ... tap ... tap ...

Seelingson's thoughts turned to Sylvia and his cold, gray eyes seemed to contract and sink further back into their deep sockets. He had given Sylvia everything; why, then, had she fallen for this incompetent, failure of a man — this Evans?

She was a beautiful and a strange woman. Always, he'd lived with the baffled feeling that he had never owned her at all. He had glimpsed in her expressive eyes, more than once, reactions toward him that angered and frustrated him, yet she never put her feelings into words, or gave him anything he could concretely fight.

He became aware that the footsteps of the man behind him were synchronized with his own. If he moved faster, they did, too; if he slowed his pace, the killer fell into step with him. The fog remained stationary; the sounds of the city were muffled. An occasional car crept cautiously through the desolate night; the dimly-lighted houses huddled in ghostly rows; everything had an eerie, unreal appearance.

HE CAME at last to the street he sought and stopped to look at a house number. The place he was hunting was two doors away; there was a light in the window. He knocked on the door It was opened by a Negro boy on crutches. Two smaller boys and a girl sat around a broken-down table in the center of a small room. His eyes, trained to quick perception, took in the faded wallpaper, the rickety wooden chairs, one with a torn cane seat, the frayed hook rug — the children staring at him with big, solemn eyes.

"You lookin' foah someone?" the boy on crutches asked.

"Yes — they told me Doctor Evans had come here."

The boy smiled in relief. "Yessuh, Doctor Evans come here tonight to bring me my new crutches." He looked down at them proudly; "now I kin git around!"

He glanced at the faces of the other

children. They were smiling now that he'd mentioned the name of Doctor Evans.

"Did he tell you where he was going?" Seelingson asked.

"Yessuh. To see Melvin Smith; he lives in the next block." The boy gave him an address.

Seelingson walked through the fog, his hands buried in his pocket. Mentally, he cursed Sylvia. The little fool! With him, she'd had everything money could buy. A lawyer, a smart lawyer, as Seelingson had been, could name his own figures, if he tied up with the right powers. All right, so he'd defended men who were murderers, racketeers — taken bribes and cheated at politics. He'd wound up with more than this skid-row medic, this Doctor Evans, hadn't he?

He'd given Sylvia things that cost more than Evans could earn in five years — Cadillacs, an apartment in the best part of town, clothes. And she wanted to swap it for a drafty flat in a skid-row tenement building, and a skinny failure of a man.

The thing had a distorted, unreal aspect that eluded Seelingson. Something he could not pin down; something that frightened him a bit. If he only had the time.

But he was carrying a little time bomb around in his belly; it was going to grow up into a full-size case of death, in a few weeks. Smarter doctors than this crummy slum district sawbones had told him that. Prognosis negative; he was walking around with a prognosis negative in his stomach.

So, Sylvia knew. So she was being discreet. She and this punk medic. They were holding back. They weren't coming out in the open with it; they were sitting around, waiting for him to die … counting the days it took.

And he did not have time to figure it out — whatever it was that made Sylvia tick; he only had time to act.

People didn't double-cross John Seelingson — especially not a woman.

He knocked on the door of the Smith home, carrying the cold, deadly anger around with him, in his guts. The door was opened by a stolid man dressed in ragged overalls. The room differed little from the one he had just left. An obese woman turned from a table, where she was stirring a spoonful of medicine into a glass of water.

Again he saw faces lighten as he inquired for Doctor Evans.

"What do you want of him?" asked the man, as he peered questioningly into Seelingson's face.

"He's needed at the hospital for an emergency case," Seelingson lied.

"It ain't for Mrs. Williams, is it?" the woman asked, grave concern in her voice.

"I don't know," Seelingson replied.

"I hope you find him, if it is," she said. "Doc Evans can save her if anyone can."

"He came to see our boy, Melvin, who had a stomach upset," the man explained. "He's a good doctor," he added. "The best," the woman said.

Seelingson mumbled thanks and turned away, abruptly.

A KIND of fury possessed him now, and he walked faster, heading for the Y.M.C.A. Hotel, where he knew Evans lived. He was eager to get the night's work

Originally published in
***Double-Action Detective Stories* #1, 1954**
Columbia Publications, Inc.

over; he wondered what Sylvia would think if she knew where he was going and what he intended to do. He could see her eyes reacting with horror. Her eyes were sounding devices for other people's thoughts and her own; he had seen many emotions expressed in them. She would never have made a good criminal lawyer for that reason … for a good mouthpiece, such as Seelingson was, never showed an emotion unless it was well-calculated to bring a reaction out of a stubborn jury.

His troubled thoughts shifted back to the footsteps behind him, in the fog. They were becoming identified with his life, like his shadow … like something sinister materialized out of the past to fulfill his present destiny.

His first idea, when he had the definite proof of Sylvia's infidelity with Evans, was to get a gun and kill them both. Then his analytical, penetrating mind took over; no — that would be too quick, too easy. A clever man like John Seelingson could plan something far more worthy of their sin.

So he had planned his own murder.

It was not hard … not with his contacts in the underworld. A little money had hired him the killer that was walking back there in the fog Funny, how little it cost to have someone murdered — even yourself.

The man knew what to do. When they found Doctor Michael Evans, the gun in the man's hand would blast the life out of John Seelingson; then the killer would quickly press the gun into the hand of the astonished Doctor Evans. He would slug Evans and phone the police. By the time they arrived, the killer would have vanished and Doctor Michael Evans would be groggily coming around, with a murdered man on the sidewalk in front of him and the murder weapon (bought in his name the day before) in his hand.

Doctor Evans, eh? How come did you knock him off, Doc?

But I didn't, I tell you!

Ever see this gun before?

No.

We found it in your hand.

I — somebody put it there. A man.

What man?

I — I don't know. He ran away.

Come now, Doctor. The gun was bought the day before John Seelingson was murdered. It's registered in your name.

But I didn't buy it! And I didn't kill him. I had no reason to kill him.

Oh, oh, now Doctor Evans! No reason? How about Sylvia? A woman is always a good reason, Doctor. Many men have killed because another man would not let a woman go. It's a motive as old as the jungle ...

Yes, it would make delightful questioning. John Seelingson only re gretted that he would not be around to enjoy it.

It was worth trading the few weeks of life remaining in his cancer-riddled body, to savor the thought of their torture.

H E CAME to the hotel at last and went quickly in. A half-dozen men were seated in the lobby; two were playing ping-pong in an alcove at the end of the room. Evans was not in sight He inquired at the desk. The elderly night clerk telephoned his room, but there was no answer.

"I saw him in the lobby a little while ago," he said. He was searching Seelingson's face. "What's the matter, mister?" he asked; "you look worried."

"Nothing's the matter."

"I hope nothing's happened to Doc Evans," said the clerk.

"Of course not," Seelingson snapped. The baffled rage was beating at him again.

"He sure is a good guy, that Doc Evans."

"He's a failure," Seelingson snapped, his tcmpcr finally breaking. "IIe was fired from the staff of the City Memorial Hospital for incompetence, did you know that?"

The room was suddenly very still.

The old clerk took a frayed match out of his mouth. "Well," he said gently, "I reckon we're all entitled to make a mistake now and then."

"Well, Evans made a good one," Seelingson said. He was shaking all over now, and the sweat was standing out in beads across his forehead. "He operated on a woman one night; emergency auto wreck. He was drunk at the time. She died. Twice he tried to start a private practice, after that, and failed both times."

The clerk looked old and sad. "Yeah," he murmured, "I knew about that; we don't talk about it much down here."

"Well you better talk about it," Seelingson swore. He wiped at his face with shaking hands. "You don't want a man like that treating you, do you? He's a lousy doctor!"

The clerk's tired old eyes drifted toward the front windows. "Folks down here ain't got much choice," he explained. "Doc Evans is the only doctor we got down here. Maybe he ain't the smartest in the world, but he's sure good to these folks. And he ain't took a drink since he's been here — over three years, now ..."

Seelingson turned and stumbled out of the hotel. He moved across the railway tracks, bumping on the ties. Across the tracks, he could see the soft lights of an all-night diner, shining through the fog. It looked warm and inviting. He started toward it; there was a cold sickness taking ahold of him.

Then the front door of the diner opened. A man came out, stood for a moment in the triangle of light. Seelingson came nearer and he saw that it was the man he had been looking for all evening. Doctor Michael Evans. The end of his quest.

Behind him, the killer's steps could

be heard again, because they were nearer now.

Tap ... tap ... tap ... tap....

Seelingson tried to stop the shaking that had come to his entire body; he was showing emotion and a good lawyer never showed emotion.

He was trying to answer questions that a good lawyer should not bother to ask himself.

What would the little colored boy on the crutch do? And the Williams woman and Melvin Smith, whose upset stomach might turn out to be appendicitis?

But these were minor questions. They hardly came to the conscious levels of his mind. He was grappling with the larger question. The one that had walked with him in the fog tonight, haunting him, never leaving him for a moment. *Why had Sylvia traded him for this failure?*

And now, painfully clear, Seelingson had the answer: He, not Dr. Michael Evans, had been the failure — in a deeper sense that he'd not seen until he came this close

to eternity. And Sylvia had never been able to stand people who were failures.

Doctor Evans was moving slowly toward him, a tired, thin man in a worn suit.

Back there, in the fog, the killer's footsteps had stopped; he was leveling the gun now. He would not miss — he was trained to do these things.

The ground began vibrating. The night express was coming down the tracks; its headlight cut through the fog.

Seelingson suddenly turned away from Doctor Evans and walked out across the tracks. Tears were streaming down his face.

He walked across the cinders and the ties and the wet rails, and the onrushing headlight impaled him for a moment. Wheels screamed on steel, and in the last possible moment, he thought that this was not so hard to take. He was giving Sylvia the first worthwhile gift in all the years he'd known her; he was giving her the man she loved. ∎

Charles Boeckman (1908-2015) contributed to magazines like *Action-Packed Western*, *Famous Detective*, *Manhunt* and *Guilty*. He led his own jazz band and authored a comprehensive jazz history. In 2009, he was awarded a star in the South Texas Music Walk of Fame in Corpus Christi, Texas. Read more of his work in *Strictly Poison and Other Stories* and *Stagecoach to Hell and Other Stories* — and autobiography *Pulp Jazz* from Bold Venture Press.

Let's Not Argue

by CONRAD ADAMSON

David pressed the numbers in rhythmic order and turned the handle to release the bolts. He reached into the safe to withdraw his service pistol and fit it inside his waistband. The corner of the slide pressing into his back reminded him that he needed to buy a better holster and that he should try bartering household chores for a backrub from his wife.

He secured the safe as his wife stepped into the garage. She tossed a flattened box into the recycling bin and gave him a frown. "Do you really need that thing? We're just going out for groceries."

"Are you going to wear your seatbelt even though you don't plan on being in a wreck?" he asked. Diana's deepened frown and wordless exit back into the house told him that his chances for a massage left with her.

David stepped in from the garage and caught his barefoot son who was running laps around the kitchen and front room.

"No daddy, I wanna play a little more!" Gavin bellowed and squirmed.

David walked Gavin to the stairs and sat the boy down next to his socks and shoes. Gavin kicked with the determination of a wild horse resisting training. "If you behave yourself you might get a cookie," David said as he worked the first sock onto the kicking foot. He gripped his son's other leg and reached for the second sock. He caught the disapproving eyes of his wife.

"Let's try not to bribe him with cookies for everything he does, I don't want him ending up like my sister."

David slipped the second sock on and eased out an exasperated breath. Where was the bright smile he remembered while she approached down the aisle under a snowy white veil? Where had the coy grin gone that he so frequently saw during their honeymoon in Tuscany? David supposed they were buried by his long hours away at work and the challenges of child rearing. He hoped they could be exhumed someday if he only had the time, energy and an idea of where to start.

After securing Gavin into his car seat, David backed out of the driveway. The subtle bump caused by the meandering crack in the pavement reminded him of his promise to Diana back in the spring that he had agreed to patch it before summer ended. The multi-colored leaves partially covering the crevice would not have been so damning if it was not the second arrival of autumn since he made the promise.

David turned at the first traffic light and glanced over to his wife. She was swiping through something on her phone as she usually did when he drove. He wasn't sure if she did this out of boredom or to avoid talking to him.

"Daddy, we can get some snacks so you have them at work tonight."

David looked at his son with the rearview mirror. "I don't have to work tonight. I'll be with you and momma all night tonight."

Gavin grinned. "Momma, daddy doesn't have to work tonight!"

Diana looked up from her phone. "That's right honey, he'll be with us all night." She gave a small smile to David before returning to her screen.

After parking David helped Gavin out of his car seat. He and Diana walked on either side of an energetic Gavin who insisted on telling him about the vampire squid he learned about on a show. In receiving Gavin's excited attention David felt the stress of work roll off his shoulders. As they reached the entrance, he saw Diana take a surreptitious glance at a muscular younger man exiting the store. David's improving mood stalled and he looked down at his own form, which made him think of a once angular sandcastle slowly melting in steady coastal rain.

David put Gavin in a cart and pushed it past the bakery. He kept his eyes away from the pastries that now filled him with more disgust for himself than temptation. At the produce, David picked up a bag of asparagus.

"Are you going to cook it this time? It went bad before we used it the last two times," Diana said.

David felt a pang of frustration but paused to decide if this was a fair point before he replied. Then he heard a sound that stole his attention. It was a sound that he usually heard muffled by earplugs, one that he never heard in a grocery store. When he heard the sound repeated twice more, he forgot completely about trying to avoid a senseless argument about vegetables with his wife.

David pulled Gavin out of the cart and

thrust him into Diana's arms. "Take Gavin and stand behind me." Diana took their son with wide eyes but made no complaint. They stepped around the corner and David drew his gun. He found the fire exit he was looking for and turned back toward his wife.

Diana's wide eyes conveyed more to David than any words she could have spoken in that moment. They told him that the core of their relationship still thrived. It told him that she didn't want to raise their child with anyone else. It told him that she also feared the eventual day when one of them would die before the other and that she feared it might already be that day because he was not leaving with her.

Over the growing sounds of running feet and screams David said, "Get out and don't call it in until you're two blocks away."

David watched Diana push through the red door with Gavin's bewildered face bobbing over her shoulder. The fire alarm activated and David turned back toward the gun shots. A young couple sprinted past him, gripping each other's hand and struggling to look behind without running into the displays ahead of them. David stepped aside to let them pass and continued forward.

He leaned his head around the dairy aisle and saw a white-haired man in a red plaid shirt. David gripped tightly and raised his gun. As he removed the slack from the trigger he was swarmed by images of birthdays, pushing Gavin on the swing, of Diana sleeping with her head on this chest. The scowling old man noticed him and swung the barrel of the rifle toward

his new target.

The slide of the pistol reared back with percussive reports that David couldn't hear. His eyes focused down to the front sight post that existed as his only pillar of salvation. It slung back and forth, waving like a tower threatening to collapse in an earthquake. It stopped with the finality of a cast die, as if it was an answer to a question waiting to be perceived.

The empty pistol magazine hit the floor as David's left hand slapped at his smooth belt where he kept the reload on his duty belt—the one secured a few miles away in a locker. As his hand continued to reflexively grope his belt for ammunition, his eyes drifted up past his empty gun.

The white hair of the killer now bore streaks of a crimson hue darker than his shirt. The crumpled body was outdone by the motion of the air, which gradually dispersed the haze and sweet acrid odor.

David looked to the locked slide of his pistol and back to the body. Despite the years of training and carrying it, he struggled in the moment to come to terms that the inanimate object he knew so well had been a tool of such effect. His right hand remained wrapped around the grip in a symbiotic embrace of opposites, of firmness and yielding, stability and chaos, intention and result. His left hand provided a more immediate puzzle as it was streaked with the same color of red that David saw in the old man's hair.

He took the panicked breath of a person falling into cold water. He jammed his gun into his holster and frantically ran his hands over his body to find the source of the bleed. The training on systematic searches for injuries was gone with all the other routine information that often disappears under the stress of a suffered gunshot.

The sting of a fingernail catching the open flap of skin on his shoulder came with a sudden surprise that washed away under the overwhelming tide of relief closely followed by a soporific fatigue. He turned so his leaning body could catch itself on the cold transparent door in front of a wide array of milk alternatives. He slid down with his arms wrapped across his chest, thinking of the protective vest that hadn't been with him to protect him when he finally needed it. He thought of the integrity of the delicate tissue of his lungs, the web of high-pressure arteries and veins guiding the systolic rush of blood within thin elastic walls, and the central coordination of it all by his heart. His heart.

The faces of Diana and Gavin returned to him and he shuddered. He tore his phone from his pocket and held his finger on the screen to speed dial his wife. Before the first ring his eyes were already clouded with tears.

"Are you alright?" Diana demanded.

"Uh-huh," David muttered, unable to articulate words through his sobbing.

"Oh my God," Diana said, trailing off and quickly matching the sound flowing into her ear.

Through the fog of emotions David couldn't see the path ahead, but he knew the path behind him. He finally understood that his life to this point was more meandering and unguided than he had ever admitted to himself openly.

But he knew he could never return to a state of mind where anything took precedence before Diana and Gavin.

They were his heart.   ■

CONRAD ADAMSON spends much of his time working while other people are in bed. During day hours he spends time with his family while pretending he isn't thinking about story ideas. Sometimes he finds a few hours to sleep. His interests outside of fiction writing include learning foreign languages, sipping Scotch, and testing the limits of what can be accomplished while listening to audiobooks. He spent his youth competing in wrestling, boxing, jiu jitsu, fencing, stick fighting, and mixed martial arts, both those days are behind him.

FACE TO INFINITY
BY E.C. TUBB

FACE TO INFINITY
First published in
New Writings in SF #28, 1976
Copyright © 1976 by E.C. Tubb
Reprinted by permission of
Cosmos Literary Agency for the
author's estate.

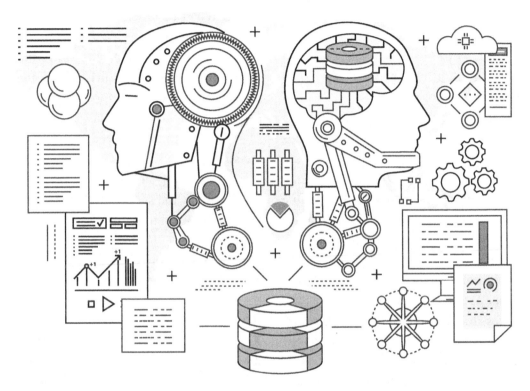

Consciousness rose like a bubble to burst in a rainbow shimmer of expanding awareness; the touch of sheets, the scent of hair, the warmth of a female body close to his own. Other things; the familiar sight of his cabin, the clock with crystal glitters, the wardrobe filled with soft fabrics. And yet more; the low susurration of voices, a murmur barely heard and still less understood.

"It must surely be obvious that for any man to suffer immolation will result in total withdrawal and inevitable insanity."

"True, but as long as the sensory perceptions are stimulated the ego will look outward, not inward. Insanity is, after all, only a matter of cultural definition."

Carter and Loomis?

He felt a sudden rage, but quickly dying out. The voices were dull; but the content was familiar. Always they argued on matters of abstruse psychology as if finding intellectual satisfaction in the mouthing of long words. And the voices could belong to no one else — they were far too deep to have belonged to the rest of the crew.

"Honey." Alice turned, waking, snuggling against him, eyes closed, hands groping like blind kittens, their touch warm and velvet. "Honey?"

"No."

"Please!"

"Up," he said. "Time to get moving."

Dressed, he entered the dining hall. Four faces looked at him, two male, two female; all rose and smiled in greeting.

"Good morning, Carl. Have a good night?"

"Sleep well?"

"You look a mite peaked, Carl. Did Alice take it out of you?"

That was Carter, round, suet-pudding of a face wreathed in a smile, pudgy hands lifting as if he were a priest giving benediction. Seated beside him Loomis, his twin, echoed the suggestive snigger. One day, Carl decided, he would do something about the pair. Something peculiarly horrible.

Alice came from behind him and took her place at the table. She was silent as she ate, eyes downcast, knowing it was time for a change and yet hating the thought of losing her favoured position. Yet it would come again, he silently promised, watching the sheen of her long, blonde hair, the curve of her cheek.

Gwen, hair as dark as midnight, spooned marmalade on toast and nibbled at the crusty morsel.

"Couldn't we increase the size of the play court?" she asked. "We could knock down one of the bulkheads and make one big room instead of two smaller ones. I'm dying for a game of tennis."

"No structural alterations of any kind are permitted," said Loomis automatically. "Be content with what you've got."

"Which is?"

"A damned sight more than anything you were used to before you joined this crew." Alice was sharp, spiteful, even white teeth flashing like those of a fox. "If you want to get rid of excess energy how about cleaning the ship?"

"Be quiet, you two!" Cynthia was a redhead and had a temper to match. "Cleaning is taken in turn. Right, Carl?"

He smiled, enjoying his supremacy, his position of power. Girls, he thought, they always like to be close to the one in authority. But he had to play fair.

"That's right," he agreed. "Alice cleans the ship. Loomis?"

"Check all systems."

"Monitor the sensors," said Carter.

Cynthia hesitated. "Void all waste matter."

"Tally the stores," said Gwen.

"Then do it," said Carl.

***

It was routine; a matter of moving from one part of the ship to another, checking, testing, seeing that everything was as it should be and that nothing had gone wrong. But nothing could go wrong — the concept was unthinkable.

Back in the recreation room they settled to take care of the rest of the day. Carter and Gwen played chess, the others made up a four at bridge. The cards were shining-clean, crisp to the fingers, the surfaces unworn.

The sound of their bids echoed like the chime of bells.

"One club," said Loomis.

"Two diamonds," said Alice.

"Three clubs," said Cynthia.

"Four no trumps," said Carl.

He won, he always won, the others

by now owed him a sum greater than the national debt. One day, perhaps, he would collect.

Bored he rose and went forward to where the great screens showed the eternal vista of the stars. For a long time he studied them, wondering how far they had come, how much further they would have to go. Years? Decades? It was possible; but what of it? They were comfortable in then — haven. The showers always ran hot and cold, the food was delicious, the company mostly pleasant and, when it wasn't, he could quickly bring it back into line.

He turned at a faint noise. Cynthia was standing just behind him, the expression in her eyes unmistakable.

"Carl," she murmured. "When is it going to be my turn again? Loomis is — " Her arms circled his body and dragged him close to her warm contours. "Carl?"

He struggled against her arms. They clutched even tighter.

"Carl!" Her voice had deepened, grown thick and demanding. The white gleam of fangs showed behind the full redness of her lips. They touched his throat, nipped, began to penetrate the skin. "I need you, Carl. I need you!"

He twisted, feeling pain at his throat, thrusting the woman from him with a jerk of his arms. For a moment the control room wheeled in a circle of brilliant glitters then it steadied and was as before.

"Carl?" The woman looked at him and was just that — a woman pleading to be loved.

"Later," he said, and walked from the place of star-bright screens and watchful dials.

He heard the murmur as he entered the recreation room. Carter and Loomis, heads together, muttering their endless litany of esoteric knowledge. They parted as he approached.

"Carl?"

"Alice," he snapped. "I want her. Where is she?"

Carter blinked. "Alice?"

"Yes, Alice, you fool!"

Loomis cleared his throat. "Carl, who is Alice?"

***

One day, thought Carl, I will kill him. I will take him and spread him out, split him down the middle and open his guts to the sky. The sky and the waiting vultures. Him and Carter both. I will get the pair of them all in my own good time.

"Alice," said Loomis. "Of course. Let's go and find her."

She wasn't to be found.

Somehow, she had vanished from the ship — but how? The tell-tales showed that no port had been opened and, anyway, they couldn't be opened from anywhere but the control room and then only after long and tedious formalities. But she wasn't in the recreation room, the dining room, the swimming pool, the showers, the kitchens, the theatre; the shooting range, the play room, the library, the laboratory, the conservatory, the observatory. She wasn't in the bedrooms, the dark room, the music room. Nor on the promenade. She had simply vanished.

Or had been made to vanish.

Carl thought about it as, the others at his heels, he strode through the echoing vastness of the ship. One or more of the others must have killed her and disposed of her body. But that too was impossible. A human body held a lot of meat, a lot of blood and bone. To pass it through the voider would take time and leave stains. There had been no time and there were no stains. Yet she could not be found.

Back in the recreation room Cynthia said, "Could something have come aboard? An invisible something from out there?" The movement of her hand signalled the great emptiness beyond the hull.

"Impossible!" Carter was firm. "If such a thing was intangible enough to pass through metal then it would have been too insubstantial to snare a human being. And, even if something could have managed to enter the ship, how could it have taken Alice out?"

"It could have dematerialized her," said Gwen. "It could have extended the matter of her material being until it had achieved a permeable tenuousness."

"That means we must have breathed in a part of her body," said Loomis. He was thoughtful. "In a sense we have incorporated her into ourselves."

"A closed, feed-back cycle," agreed Carter. "She is us and we are her. That means we must all share her appetite. Shall we eat?"

"No," said Carl.

He was, naturally, obeyed.

***

That evening Cynthia died.

It was evening only by convention, there was no real time aboard the vessel, but the habit of regular hours was a psychological necessity in order to maintain the workings of the biological clock. Carl heard the scream, the thick slobbering giggle, saw the horror as he burst into the kitchen.

Gwen stood over a moaning figure, a knife in her hand. As she saw him she stooped and plunged it into Cynthia's body. A fountain of blood spurted from the ripped abdomen, staining her dress, painting her face into a devil's mask. Giggling she threw aside the knife and draped her neck with smoking entrails. Kneeling she thrust her face into the puddle of blood oozing from the gaping wound.

"My God!" Carter turned away, retching. "No! No, I didn't mean — for God's sake do something!"

"It has all been taken care of." Loomis, with his bland, hateful face, his too-ready smile. "The trauma will not last and soon the conviction that all is normal will overwhelm the sense of disorientation. There is no need for concern."

Carl knocked him aside, slamming the kitchen door and locking it as he cut off the sight of the horror within. Sweating he stood against the panel, heard the thud from the other side, doubled as pain lanced his side to blur his vision with spinning darkness. Dimly he heard the thick, inhuman voice, snarling an impotent rage.

"I'll get you! I'll get you if it's the last thing I do! You won't get away with this, damn you! You sadistic perverts! You monsters! You filthy, degenerate swine! I'll make you pay for what you've done to me!"

His voice, and then another, cool, hatefully calm.

"Steady now, Carl. Just relax and take it easy."

Carter stood before him, smiling, something bright and shining in his hand. He lifted it, aimed, thrust it directly into Carl's neck. Pain from the lacerated throat merged with the dull agony in his side. He tried to run and fell to lie sprawled on the floor looking up at the two men.

"An expected reaction," said Loomis with chill detachment.

"Beneficial?"

"Unfortunately, no, but it will pass. Everything will pass. A hundred years from now and all will be forgotten."

"Damn you!" Carl climbed painfully to his feet. His legs felt numb, dead, appendages without feeling or function. He blinked to clear his eyes of crystal glitters, feeling a new terror. "The ship!" he gasped. "Something is wrong with the ship!"

Loomis smiled, his head shrinking, to grow round and studded with eyes. His body dropped, sprouted legs, grew a thick, ugly covering tufted with sparse fur. On multiple legs the spider scuttled up the wall to hang watching with glittering eyes.

"Carter!" He turned to the other man. "Help me, damn you. Help me!"

"To do what, Carl?"

"To get out of here, man. What else? To get out of here!"

Solemnly Carter shook his head.

"I'm afraid that is quite impossible, Carl. After all you did volunteer, and surely this is better than spending your life in a cell? Five years, perhaps less, and you will be free. Just five, short years. And you will not suffer, I promise you that."

"You bastard! I didn't know. I didn't guess! For God's sake get me out of here!"

He ran from the empty smile, racing through endless corridors, endless rooms, running until the breath rasped in his lungs and his muscles trembled with exhaustion. Finally he halted to stare at a black loathsome body, a smiling mask which gently swayed from side to side.

"I told you," said Carter. "It is quite impossible to escape. Now why not be sensible and make the best of things? The connections are all made and cannot be unmade. And think of the adventure!"

"You said five years?"

"Maybe a little more; but it will be your time, Carl, not ours. We shall all be dead by then. But you will be expected and science will have progressed far enough then to do what we cannot. So have hope, my friend. Hope ... hope ... hope ... "

Hope!

The name of the ship.

The only thing left to him.

The only promise to be found in a universe of pain and terror, the machinations of science and the bleakness of despair.

To hope and to continue hoping for now and forever.

But first must come revenge.

He flung himself at the smiling face, hands reaching to rip and tear, to maim and to kill. Beneath his hands Carter moaned and then began to melt, to fall and end in a thin, oozing mat of slime on the floor. From the slime lifted a hundred grasping hands, a thousand sprouting eyes, ten thousand gaping mouths all gusting an acrid vapour.

Blinded, terrified, he ran from the scene, slammed into a bulkhead, turned and again met the stunning impact of unyielding metal. When next he threw himself forward he felt the bite of strands about his limbs, the constricting material of a web holding him close, closer, binding him tight until he could hardly breathe and found it impossible to move.

On the wall the spider moved, swinging from side to side, spinning, becoming a blurred circle of eye-bright glitters which grew and grew until there was nothing in the universe but the overwhelming, hypnotic shimmer.

Carl groaned and looked at the thing just above his face, at the wheeling points of light, bright and clean in their random motion. He could see, in the reflection of the stainless steel eighteen inches above, the lined and ravaged face, the complex helmet with the trailing wires, the pipes buried in his arms and throat, the thick cables sprouting from the support cradling his head.

The cables wired into the "dead" areas of his brain, the nine tenths for which the only use was to function now as the living computer of the ship. His ship. The *Hope* of which he was the guiding part.

The probe sent out to circle a distant star and to return to Earth — one day.

Rolling his eyes he could see, just to one side, the cause of the breakdown. Drifting globules had already sealed the tiny hole but the damage had been done. A tiny meteor had penetrated the hull and smashed the dream-mechanism on which his sanity depended.

Now there would be no more dreams, no women, no company, no illusion of space and gracious living.

There would be nothing but the endless years in which, locked in a metal coffin, he would go inevitably and totally insane.

But he wouldn't die. The machines would see to that.   ∎

English writer **EDWIN CHARLES TUBB** is internationally known, having been translated into more than a dozen languages. Born in London in 1919, he lived there until his death in 2010. In a sixty-year writing career he published over 120 novels, and 200 science fiction short stories in such magazines as *Astounding/Analog, Authentic, Galaxy, Nebula, New Worlds, Science Fantasy,* and *Vision of Tomorrow.*

Some of his finest sf short stories were collected in *The Best Science Fiction of E.C. Tubb* (Wildside, 2003). Tubb continued to write dynamic new science fiction novels right up to his death; his final novel, *Fires of Satan,* was published by Gollancz in 2013. New editions of his novels and collections of his best short stories continue to be published posthumously, and all of his books have remained constantly in print.

CODE NAME:
INTREPID

CASE GRAY

BY ROBERT J. MENDENHALL

I.

Another Body

The body lay sprawled over the Delaware beach, its face distorted into a mask of fear and agony. Its arms and fingers stretched outward like claws locked in rigor and desperate to keep something terrible at bay. But it was the mottled flesh of the face and the rancid odor wafting from it that left even the police detective white and shaky. Lieutenant Colonel Rick Justice knelt in the sand and studied the corpse, unaffected.

"I don't know why they called in the Army Air Corps," said the pale detective. "My department can handle this." His words were hollow, meant to bolster his own confidence and nothing more. He knew full well this was beyond his experience.

Justice stood and faced the policeman. "I'm sure of it, Detective." His deep voice, smooth as syrup, coated the policeman with reassurance. Justice had that effect on men, the ability to deliver confidence with only his voice. And women? Women who heard him speak for the first time often forgot their own names.

Justice removed his uniform cap to reveal a thick shock of hair the color of summer wheat, cut precisely to military regulation. At several inches over six feet, he stood a head taller than the detective. Eyes blue as a noon sky looked over firm cheek bones and a square jaw. His shoulders were broad, rounded, and solid, bulging beneath the khaki uniform shirt. His chest strained against the material, as did his substantial arms.

Dozens of War Department personnel go missing! Codename: Intrepid discovers an insidious plot to create an army of undead soldiers. This one has it all — Nazis, aerial dog-fights — and zombies!

The detective nodded, accepting the statement with relief. "You made it here rather quickly, Colonel. I'm surprised."

"I was already in the area," Justice told him. He did not mention that he had been called out hours earlier by Assistant Secretary of War Harry Hines Woodring, when a body in this very condition had been found farther up the coast. That body had been the third in two days. This was the fourth.

"I'll need the body taken to the Annapolis Medical Center. Can you arrange that?" Justice asked.

"In Maryland? Sure, but that's almost four hours away, Sacred Heart Memorial is closer."

"One of my team is on staff at Annapolis," said Justice.

"Your team?"

Justice did not reply. He focused on a dark shape, far out over the ocean.

"Ah, sure," the detective said. "I can arrange that for you."

"See to it that no one else has contact with the body. It is imperative no one but trained medical staff touches it. Especially the exposed skin--"

The detective jerked back, falling onto his backside. His pale face was now bleach white, his eyes round as nickels. His jaw hung open nearly to his heaving chest.

"D-did you… did you s-see?" the detective wheezed.

"See what?' Justice asked with deliberate calm.

The detective pointed a trembling finger

ROBERT J. MENDENHALL is a retired police officer, retired Air National Guardsman, and former Broadcast Journalist for the American Forces Network, Europe. A member of Science Fiction and Fantasy Writers of America and Mystery Writers of America, he writes in multiple genres. Recently, his historical story "War Torn" was featured at SaturdayEveningPost.com. His short fiction has appeared in three *Star Trek: Strange New Worlds* anthologies published by Pocket Books, and anthologies by Chaosium Publishing, Local Hero Press, Nomadic Delirium Press, Rogue Star Press, and Dark Alley Press. Airship 27 recently released a collection of his *Code Name: Intrepid* stories.

Robert lives in southwestern Michigan with his wife and fellow writer, Claire. And many animals. So many animals …

Visit his web site: RobertJMendenhall.com, follow him on Twitter: @robtjmendenhall, or send him an e-mail: robert@robertjmendenhall.com.

at the corpse. "He… it moved."

Justice looked at the inanimate body, then back at the policeman. "He's dead, Detective. He couldn't have moved."

The police detective scampered backward like a crab, kicking up sand in his wake. "T-then what do you call that?"

Justice looked stone-faced at the corpse. He watched as its left arm twitched. Then its right. The dead man's eyes popped open, their oily pupils clouded and blank. The corpse grunted a hungry snarl, like a wild animal circling its prey. It sat up in a jerky motion, twisted its torso until it was erect. The odor that wafted from its gaping mouth was pungent as rotting fish.

"Can you understand me?" Justice asked the animated corpse.

It gave no indication of understanding, but looked blankly past him, its putrid breath short and shallow.

Justice circled the dead man, observing every angle of the body, noting every blotch and each dry wound. If a dead man suddenly coming to life had startled or frightened Rick Justice, he gave no indication of it.

The detective was back on his shaky feet. "What the hell is happening?"

"Do you know where you are?" Justice asked as he angled back into the corpse's line of sight. It continued to stare unblinkingly past him with eyes devoid of color.

Justice recognized the distinctive sound of metal on leather. He turned toward it as the detective drew his service revolver from his hip holster and leveled the handgun at the dead man in a trembling, two-handed grip.

"Don't," Justice said, his voice now rigid steel.

The detective fired at the re-animated corpse. The bullet tore through its left arm. Blood, grainy and the color of dirty rust, splattered the sand. The body snarled. It turned its head in a cock-eyed roll. It thrashed upright, its arms swinging in a rage.

"Stop," Justice commanded.

Neither the dead man nor the detective complied.

Four more shots tore into the chest of the corpse as it flailed toward the detective.

Another shot and a click-click-click from the revolver.

A guttural wail from the corpse. A bellow of fear from the detective.

As the corpse's scaly hands came within inches of the detective's throat, another shot rang out, this one an explosion compared to the pop of the revolver. The 45-caliber bullet tore into the side of the body's head, blasting an exit wound that ruptured much of its face and skull. It sank to the sand like limp laundry.

Rick Justice holstered his pistol.

The police captain stared wide-eyed at the corpse. "Is … is it dead?"

"Yes. It is still dead." Justice knelt beside the body and methodically searched its pockets. In the inside jacket pocket, he found something interesting.

A soldier who had been waiting for Justice at the top of the bluff now raced toward them sideways down the steep grade.

"Sir, I heard shots," the soldier called out. "Are you …" The sight of the bloody, nearly faceless body, stopped the soldier in his tracks.

"We're fine, Corporal." Justice stood

and pocketed his discovery. "The detective is going to arrange for an ambulance. I want you to take the car and follow the body to Annapolis Medical Center. Make sure nothing happens to it along the way. It is to be turned over to Doctor Steven Lester and no one else."

"Yes, sir," said the corporal. "But what about you?"

The sound of an engine, high-pitched and revving fast, resounded from the ocean. The detective looked out, expecting to see a speedboat heading toward shore. What he saw instead made his jaw drop. It was a boat, all right. A flying boat.

"What in heaven's name…" the detective said as he stared at the queer craft angling though the sky. It cut into the surface of the water, the sharply angled keel slicing through waves in a neat cleave. The gulls scattered, screeching in protest.

It looked like a boat. It *was* a boat; the detective was sure of it. But it had a significant tailfin, and a long wing mounted laterally across the closed hull and attached to the boat's sides by pylons. Small pontoons protruded from the wing at each end, skimming through the water. A pair of huge motors was mounted on the wing's leading edge.

First a walking dead man, the detective thought. Then a flying boat. What next? "What *is*

that?" the detective asked.

"That is a Consolidated Aircraft XPY-1 *Catalina*. A prototype flying boat the Navy is considering."

"The Navy? Aren't you Army?" the detective asked. He looked back at the *Catalina*. "What's it doing here?"

"It's here to pick me up," Justice replied. He walked past the detective and waded into the surf as the *Catalina* bobbed its way to shore. The gulls regrouped safely away from the strange flying machine. The faraway dark shape changed direction.

"Pick you…" The detective let the exclamation fade as he watched, open-jawed, as the flying boat slowed and a side hatch opened. "Just who the devil are you?"

The twin engines wound down to a low pitch, but did not stop. A man's head popped out of the open hatch.

It was an unusual head, large and square, with wiry hair the color of clean copper. The face below was equally unusual, eyes large and round with pupils nearly the same shade of metal as the hair. The nose was squat and pugged as if more than once it had been struck by a fist. Thin lips were wide in a grin, exposing teeth that were uneven and more ivory tan than white. The skin was coarse and pock-marked.

"Need a lift, Colonel?" the coarse man said over the twin-engine roar. His voice was a gravelly baritone, not at all incongruous with his rough appearance.

Justice said nothing. He removed his service cap, angled around the wing, and took the offered hand. Once he was inside, the coarse man secured the hatch. Justice slipped sideways past him and dropped into the right-hand co-pilot's seat.

"Secured," the coarse man—Gunnery Sergeant Dexter "Guns" Preston, United States Marine Corps--called up to the pilot.

"Strap in, Guns," the pilot answered.

The pilot—Lieutenant Commander

Roger "Sky Hawk" Winchester, United States Navy, was a tall, lean-muscled man in his late thirties. His hair bordered between bark brown and rust red, depending on the light. He wore a Clark Gable mustache above a perpetual grin. His cheeks were prominent, his jaw round and his chin cleft. His complexion, while not as abrasive as Preston's, had the weathered texture of a man who spent a great deal of time in the wind.

His eyes were his most noticeable feature. They were sparkling and bright emerald, not the dull hazel of most green-eyed people. When you looked at him, you looked right into those eyes. You couldn't help it. Winchester often used that to his advantage.

Guns and Sky Hawk were members of a special team, code name: Intrepid. Administrative supervision of Intrepid was the responsibility of the War Department Office of Special Actions. Overall accountability was to the assistant secretary of war. Command and leadership of Intrepid rested with Rick Justice.

"Airstrip, Colonel?" Winchester asked, glancing at Justice.

"Not yet," Justice replied as he strapped himself into the co-pilot's seat. "Follow the coast south a bit."

Winchester didn't question the order. He deftly pivoted the *Catalina* through the water, primed the throttle, and goosed the engines. The flying boat gathered speed, bouncing and skipping over waves. In a surprisingly short distance, it sprang into the air and thrust upward at a sixty-degree angle.

"Guns," Justice called over the din of the engines. "Fire up the fifty."

Preston unstrapped his belt and leaned between the pilots' seats, grinning. "Trouble, Colonel?"

"Bogey at our eight o'clock. I spotted him on the beach. He's been keeping a distance, but not anymore. He's heading right this way."

"Hot damn," Guns shouted as he pushed off and bolted for the rear of the craft.

Winchester craned over his left shoulder and spotted the approaching aircraft. "Can't make out what it is. Can you, Colonel?"

"It's a Fokker D VII."

Winchester shot a glance at Justice, half-expecting the Air Corps ace to be joking. But Justice rarely joked. He was serious. "How can you…?"

"I caught a brief silhouette on the beach. It was enough for me to make out the staggered wing configuration, open cockpit, and one head."

Winchester looked back at the rapidly closing airplane. He could barely recognize it from this distance. How could Justice have seen and categorized it from so far away, and so quickly?

Preston opened an overhead hatch and cranked up a telescoping mount. Atop the mount was a Browning air-cooled fifty-caliber machine gun. It was one of the many modifications Justice had made to the *Catalina*'s design. Preston dropped heavy-gauged goggles over his eyes, climbed through the hatch, fed the ammo strap through the weapon, and pulled back on the charging handle.

"Set," Preston shouted.

"Let's see who they are," Justice said. "Come about, Hawk."

"Aye, aye, Colonel."

Winchester banked the aircraft up and over, setting a speeding course nearly dead-on to the approaching airplane. The engines roared. Winchester pushed the *Catalina* faster and faster.

Preston thumbed the safety off.

Twin Spandau 7.92 mm machine guns, mounted to the Fokker's fuselage and synchronized to the rotation of its propeller, spat flaming bullets at the *Catalina*. The shots narrowly missed them, their trajectory restricted by the bi-plane's flight path.

"Holy smoke, Hawk! Watch your flyin'," Preston yelled.

"This isn't a fighter plane, Guns," Winchester called back as he banked away from the bi-plane. "It's a bathtub with wings!"

The *Catalina*'s Browning didn't have the same line-of-flight restriction as the Fokker's weapons. Preston swiveled the fifty, lining the forward sight well ahead of the bi-plane's course. He depressed the trigger. The Browning belched.

Preston's aim was true. The stream of bullets shredded the bi-plane's fabric-and-wood upper wing and fuselage. Smoke spewed from the engine's side vents. The Fokker tilted right and careened toward the water. The *Catalina* banked up and away from the spiraling bi-plane, then angled around.

The bi-plane hit the water at a sharp angle, breaking up in a spray of ocean. The bulk of it, heavy with the plane's engine and sheet metal cowling, sank quickly in a cauldron of foam and spilled fuel.

"No chutes," Winchester said as he circled the debris. "And no body. Pilot went down with it."

"The plane didn't have any markings. Any idea who they were, Colonel?" Preston asked as he lowered the Browning and secured the hatch.

The colonel set his jaw, but he did not reply.

II.

At the Air Strip

Thirty minutes later, the *Catalina*'s retractable landing wheels touched down on the sole runway of Ingold Airstrip. A decommissioned air field formerly used as a training base by the old United States Army Air Service toward the end of the Great War, the strip was now the base of operations for Justice's special team, code name: Intrepid.

A door-less utility truck, its windshield folded forward on its hood and its bulky tires spraying dirt and gravel, sped toward the *Catalina*. Behind the wheel of the vehicle sat a short, barrel-chested man, bald-headed, with a flowing handlebar mustache, waxed to a licorice gloss and clearly not regulation. His jowls were round and gave the impression of an extra chin. The shirt sleeves of his sweat-stained khaki uniform were rolled up above his beefy forearms. He gripped the steering wheel with fingers each as thick as a roll of quarters.

Master Sergeant Michael "Hammer" Downe, United States Army, was Intrepid's resident mechanic. There was no known engine in any land, sea, or air vehicle he could not fix.

The truck fishtailed to a dusty stop mere feet from the *Catalina* as its three passengers jumped out. Hawk and Guns secured the flying boat to the tarmac. Justice approached Hammer.

"Woodring has been burning up the wireless, Colonel," Hammer told Justice as the colonel slipped into the front passenger seat of the utility vehicle. Hammer clutched, slipped the gear directly into second, and crushed the accelerator pedal to the floorboard. He popped the clutch and the vehicle jerked forward, again spraying dust and gravel. Everyone knew that the assistant secretary of war was not a patient man; it wouldn't to do keep him waiting any longer.

The utility vehicle slid to a stop in front of a squat wooden building no bigger than a filling station. The siding was covered in drab olive paint that had faded and peeled over the years to reveal the original cedar beneath. The windows were painted over, and the roof was a patchwork of plywood and shingles. The entire structure looked as if it would collapse in on itself at the slightest breeze.

They jumped from the utility vehicle, bounded up the three wood-slat stairs to the rickety door, and pushed it inward. The room before them was small and dark, the only illumination from slices of light sneaking between the streaks of paint on the windows. The floor beneath their dusty boots creaked under their weight. In three steps, Hammer had crossed the room and slipped a thick key into the rusty lock of another door. The door popped open with a whisper. Hammer pulled it wide and motioned for Justice to precede him down the flight of steel stairs leading to the lower level

"After you, Colonel," Hammer said with a flourish of his hand.

Justice nodded and took the steps two at a clip, his heavy footfalls on the metal stairs echoing down the narrow stairway. At the bottom stood another door, this one metal like the stairs. There was no lock. Justice pushed down on the handle. The door swung silently inward, revealing a brightly lit room easily ten times the size of the dilapidated building above it.

The walls and the ceiling were rock and mortar reinforced by steel beams, making the underground room a bunker able to withstand a direct bombardment. This was one of the many modifications Justice had made to the old airstrip once it was turned over to him for Intrepid.

Oak desks and tables laden with equipment lined the walls. One wall was covered in maps. In the middle of the room, under a series of bright incandescent bulbs, a massive round table stood, empty now as were the dozen metal and foam chairs that surrounded it.

A woman sat behind one of the oak desks. She looked up at their approach, stood, and faced them.

"Rick," she purred. Her voice and tone were sultry and expectant. She looked at Rick Justice with unabashed admiration-- and perhaps hopeful expectation.

"Hello, Rita," Justice said evenly, his syrupy voice enveloping her.

Rita's demeanor hardened at his neutral reply. She reined in her emotions and became what she was best at. All business.

Rita Marshall was a lean, athletic woman not bound by the expectations of her generation, much to the dismay of her father. Rear Admiral James Marshall, United States Navy, expected all his daughters to behave properly--meaning tend to their men, tend to their homes, and mind their own business. Rita would have none of that. She rode horses, climbed mountains, and held a college degree. She was a brilliant scientist and avid adventuress, and would have joined the military herself if women had been allowed in. But not the Navy. She would have joined the Army just to annoy her father.

"Right," she said. "Secretary Woodring has been on the wireless for an hour, wondering where you were and if you had made confirmation."

"Rita," Justice said. "Please transmit to Secretary Woodring that Intrepid is gathered and we will be leaving within the hour."

"Leaving?" she asked. "For where?"

"Please send that," said Justice. Rita nodded slightly, then turned back to the wireless.

"Hammer," Justice said. "Pre-flight the *Liberty*."

"Roger, sir," Downe said, then bounced toward the door.

"Why the air ship, Rick?" Winchester asked. "It's slow."

Justice stepped over to the map wall and lowered a chart of the Atlantic seaboard.

"Body one was found here." He pointed to a spot on the New Jersey shoreline. "Body two here. Three here. And four here. The Atlantic current west of the Gulf Stream follows the shoreline from north to south, so it's safe to assume those bodies went into the ocean north of body one."

"Makes sense," Winchester said. "But from where?"

Justice selected another map, this one a chart of the New York, New Jersey, and Delaware coastline.

"We encountered the Fokker approximately here," Justice said, placing a finger on this new map. "The estimated range of the Fokker D VII at its maximum cruising speed of 124 miles per hour is 186 miles. The point of no return would be 93 miles." Justice drew a crude circle on the chart. "This is our search area."

At that moment, another member of the Intrepid team entered the bunker. The man was tall and thin. The lenses of his glasses were as thick as the bottoms of Coca Cola bottles. His skin was pallid as flour. Wire-thin charcoal hair barely covered his skull.

"You were right, Colonel," the bespectacled man said. He strode to the center table stiffly (a result of him needing to wear leg braces, having contracted polio as a child) and dropped several sheets of bond paper onto it. This was Professor Lucius "Glasses" Wellington, PhD., a tenured professor at Princeton University currently on sabbatical.

"What do you mean, Glasses?" Preston asked.

"Colonel?" Wellington deferred to Justice.

"I found a medallion in the pocket of the dead man we encountered this morning." Justice laid the circle medallion on the table, and all gathered around it. It was gold press and about the size of a pocket watch. In the center of the medallion was a series of crossed lines, angled at 90 degrees from each other. A scroll of ornate text encircled the crossed lines: *Nationalesozialistische Deutsche Arbeiterpartei.*

"National Socialist German Workers Party," Justice translated.

"Nazis," Glasses Wellington added.

Justice flipped the coin over. The back side was textured with brush strokes and engraved with two words in German. "*Fall Grau*," Justice said.

"My German is a little rusty, Rick," Winchester asked.

"Fall Grau translates to Case Gray," Justice said.

"Case Gray? What is that?" Rita asked.

"I believe," Justice replied, "it refers to a large-scale operation involving the reanimation of corpses."

"Zombies?" Rita asked.

Wellington said, "The four bodies were all civilian employees of the War Department, recently reported missing. According to Secretary Woodring, there are a total of thirty-two missing employees."

"Thirty-two?" Winchester said. "Only four bodies have turned up."

"There's more," Wellington said. "The last body, the one that you shot, Colonel. He was working for the Bureau of Investigation."

"I suspected as much when I found the medallion. I believe he was trying to get information about Case Gray to the War Department," Justice explained. "Where were the other missing civilians from?"

Wellington shuffled through the sheets of bond paper and removed one from the stack. "All were assigned to the Johnsburg Arsenal in upstate New York."

"All?" Winchester asked. "Why wasn't it reported?"

"Johnsburg is a remote ammunition depot with no telephone service, and there are often long periods of time with no com-munication in or out," Justice explained.

"You think we'll find them there?" Preston asked, pointing to the search area Justice had circled on the map.

"I believe so. If they are still alive."

"Or dead and alive again," Preston added.

"Oh, that reminds me, Colonel," Glasses said. "Dr. Lester telephoned the bunker while you were on the way here. It seems that the first dead body he was examining suddenly sat up on the autopsy table. The doc wasn't happy."

"What about the other two?" Justice asked.

"He said one woke up in the freezer, and he cut the head off the other before it reanimated."

"Enough chit-chat. When do we leave?" Rita interrupted.

"Not *we*, Rita," Justice said. "You're not coming with us."

Winchester and Preston shot a knowing glance at each other and grinned. This was an old argument. And the only time they ever saw Rick Justice lose.

"If you think I'm going to sit down here and take dictation like some secretary just because I'm a woman, you have another thing coming, Colonel Justice. I'm every bit as capable of handling trouble as any of your glory-boys. And I'm twice the fighter as that illiterate, foul-smelling, thick-skulled jarhead."

"Hey, who's thick-skulled?" Preston asked with mock indignation. Rita Marshall could call him anything she wanted.

"Rita—"

"Don't 'Rita' me," she said as she marched toward the door. "I'll see you on

The Liberty crisscrossed the search area. For thirty minutes, five periscopes scanned the sea and sky ...

the *Liberty*."

Her long, auburn hair flowed behind her like a cape. The sway of her hips beneath the contour-hugging khaki trousers was hypnotic. As she passed Preston, the trailing wake of her Bellodgia Caron perfume made his knees slightly weak; its hints of vanilla and clove stayed with him long after her footfalls on the metal stairs echoed away.

"When are you going to give that up, Rick?" Sky Hawk Winchester asked.

Justice ignored him.

III.

Aboard the Liberty

The *Liberty* glided away from the strip under the cover of a cloud. This was no ordinary cloud, however. It was artificially created by a complex contraption of Rick Justice's design. The apparatus created an electrically-charged layer of smoke that was vented through the *Liberty*'s outer skin, where it clung to the airship's specially designed covering, giving it the appearance of a thick cumulus cloud. The color of the smoke could be altered from white to gray relative to the electrical charge, and the thickness of the cloud could be varied based on the amount of moisture distilled from the surrounding air. It worked best in high humidity, when moisture was abundant,

but the *Liberty* carried a 1,000-gallon water tank to augment the atmosphere in low-humidity conditions.

The Cloud Cover allowed the *Liberty* to travel and hover virtually unseen.

Sky Hawk Winchester sat at the pilot controls in the flight compartment of the *Liberty*'s passenger gondola, and deftly guided the dirigible northeastward toward the Atlantic. The rest of the team huddled around a long conference table in the operations compartment, just aft of flight. Before them lay the map of the Atlantic seaboard Justice had taken from the bunker, along with sheets of graph paper scribbled and slashed with calculations. Once aloft, Justice had been able to further reduce the search area by overlaying the range limitation of the Fokker with the sea-current patterns and the locations of the beached bodies.

"We have about two hours until sunrise," Justice told them. The hatch between flight and operations was open so Winchester could hear. The team listened intently. "And about an hour- and-a-half before the sky is light enough to see below us. Once we get into the search area, I want each of you at a periscope. We'll be looking for a very large vessel or a small island, anything that would be big enough for an airplane to land on.

"I want to stress that we have three objectives. First and foremost, this is a rescue mission. There are at least twenty-eight hostages from Johnsburg Arsenal, maybe more. Second, we need to learn what the Nazis are up to. Third, we need to stop it. By any means. Any questions?"

There were none.

"Activate the Cloud Cover," Justice ordered Glasses.

"I'm on it," Wellington said. He pivoted and hobbled to the far end of the operations compartment and the Cloud Cover apparatus control panel. He adjusted the electromagnetic charge level and the moisture output, then pulled down on a contact lever. A low hum emanated from behind the panel, followed by a series of high-pressure hisses all up and down the length of the air ship. Within minutes, the *Liberty* was totally enveloped in a grayish cloud.

They entered the search area just as the first rays of the morning sun broached the horizon. Justice ordered the periscopes lowered. Unlike periscopes on Navy submarines, which were raised above the surface of the water, the *Liberty*'s periscopes were lowered to protrude just below the Cloud Cover. Each periscope could be rotated a full 360 degrees, to provide the complete picture of what was below and around the airship.

The *Liberty* crisscrossed the search area. For thirty minutes, five periscopes scanned the sea and sky, observing nothing but empty waves and cloudy skies. An hour passed. And another. And they continued to search.

At the third hour, Justice left his scope and returned to the conference table in silence. He spread his maps and charts, and recalculated.

"You think the Colonel made a mistake?" Downe whispered to Preston.

"Not a chance," Preston said in a soft voice he hoped Justice could not hear. "If he says it's here, then it's here."

"Okay," Downe replied.

Justice leaned on the table, hovering over his math.

"Wait a minute," Rita said, her forehead pushed hard against the rubber eyepiece. "Wait…"

"What is it, Rita?" Justice asked.

"Boys, take a look. Below and at 7 o'clock."

Justice returned to his scope and rotated until he was pointed in the right direction.

"What do you see, Rita?" Preston asked.

"That large cloud," she said.

"Ah, which cloud? The sky is full of them."

"The one below and at 7 o'clock, Guns," she said.

"All I see is a big cloud."

"Moron," Rita exclaimed. "It's not moving."

"She's right," Justice said. "The surrounding clouds are all in motion. That one is not."

"Big enough to hide a small island," Wellington noted.

"Hawk," Justice called into the flight compartment. "Take us down slowly. Station-keeping right above that cloud layer."

"Aye, aye, Colonel," Winchester called back.

Gradually the *Liberty* sank, until the bottom of her cover brushed the upper layer of the cloud.

"Lower scopes to maximum," Justice ordered.

Each of the five periscopes telescoped to their limits.

"All I see is more cloud," Downe said.

"Drop another ten feet," Justice said, "but no more. Our electromagnetic charge keeps our prop wash from dissipating our Cloud Cover. Not so with that cloud. I don't want to blow it away."

The *Liberty* dropped slowly another ten feet and held. One by one, the wispy clouds in their periscopes' apertures thinned, and they saw what they had been searching for. It was small as islands go, little more than a potato-shaped hunk of rock protruding from the ocean, devoid of vegetation or shore. An airstrip ran the length of the island, cleaving it in two. On the south half stood a single hangar and a series of maintenance buildings. A lone, window-less structure sat on the north half. It was a cigar box the size of a football field, with a single door at ground level facing the runway. A solitary hatch on the graveled roof suggested access.

"This is it," Justice said smoothly. "Stick to the plan. And remember, if you encounter a zombie--"

"Zombie?" Preston asked.

"You'll know one if you see one. It's a walking corpse, so remember it's already dead. The only way to stop it is with a head shot. Understood?"

They all understood.

"Hawk, take us up and over the leeward side of the runway. Then put the *Liberty* at station-keeping."

"Aye aye, Colonel," Winchester called from the flight compartment.

"Hammer, prep the auto-gyros."

"On it," Downe said, and both he and Glasses bounded out of the operations compartment toward the *Liberty*'s interior hangar.

"Air ship at station-keeping, Rick," Winchester said as he stepped through the hatch into operations.

"On your way, then."

"Let's go, Guns," Winchester said.

IV.

Onto the Island

Hawk sat at the controls of a modified Boeing F4B fighter. Guns was strapped into the rearward-facing second seat, already adjusting the ammunition feed of the tripod-mounted Browning machine gun. The bi-plane was attached to a telescoping trapeze by an eye-hook mounted to its upper wing. The hatch below the plane was already open to the sky, and the noises of the open air and the *Liberty*'s engines filled the hangar.

Justice edged along the narrow gangway past the F4B and exchanged a quick, casual salute with Winchester. Ahead of him, strapped into the first single-seat open-cockpit auto-gyro, Hammer Downe was securing the two Thompson sub-machine guns he had grabbed from the weapons locker to the rack at his side. He wore twin shoulder holsters, each packed with Smith and Wesson .45-caliber semi-automatic pistols. He nodded as Justice passed him.

Rita Marshall was, likewise, securing

a machine gun to her auto-gyro.

Justice slipped into the third auto-gyro and strapped himself in. He secured his own machine gun, adjusted the extra clips and hand grenades in his over-sized trouser pockets, and checked the strap on his hip holster. He signaled Wellington.

Glasses limped over toward Justice's craft and leaned over the rail from the gangway.

Justice had to shout over the wind noise. "Glasses, once we're away, stand by the cargo gondola. Lower it only at my flare. Your primary concern is keeping the *Liberty* safe until I signal you. If it looks like the air ship is in danger, get it away from the island."

"Understood, Colonel," Wellington called back. "Good luck."

"Let's move," Justice said.

Wellington pushed off the rail and hobbled back up the gangway. At the F4B, he flashed a thumbs-up to Winchester. Winchester nodded and adjusted his goggles. Preston did the same. Wellington backed up to the trapeze control and pulled several levers. With a clacking of metal on metal, the trapeze lowered the bi-plane through the open hatch.

Once clear of the *Liberty*, Winchester cranked the engine and it sputtered to life. At that, he pulled a handle on the control panel and the eye-hook holding the plane to the trapeze opened. The F4B dropped a quick thirty feet. Winchester opened the throttle, the engine whined, and the plane shot down and forward.

Wellington stepped away from the periscope and signaled Justice that Winchester was away. Justice jabbed a finger in the

air and whirled it. Wellington opened the hatches beneath the three auto-gyros. Air rushed into the hangar full-force.

Winchester cleared the Cloud Cover, banking up and away from the camouflaged *Liberty* in a wide arc.

He opened the throttle wide. The plane's engine screamed.

Winchester dove straight for the runway, thumbing the triggers mounted to the half-wheel in a strafing run. Bullets tore at the pavement, spewing bits of gravel and dust and making a great deal of noise.

At the end of the runway, he banked sharply over the hangar.

Guns opened up on the hangar with the Browning as they passed, ripping holes in the roof and shattering windows along its side.

As they banked and prepared for another run, the hangar doors opened and three Fokker D VII bi-planes were pushed out onto the runway. The hangar looked as if it could only hold four, possibly five planes, and they had already shot one down along the Delaware coast.

"Here we go," Sky Hawk shouted over his shoulder to Preston.

All three Fokkers were airborne within half a minute. Winchester goosed the throttle and shot away fast and furious, the Fokkers in pursuit.

Wellington turned away from his periscope and waved at Justice, who nodded. Wellington pulled three levers in succession and the trapezes securing the auto-gyros lowered though the opening.

Once outside and clear of the air ship,

they engaged their overhead rotary wings. As the blades spun faster and faster, the whine progressed into a high-pitched song. All three adjusted their goggles and ear-pads.

Justice released first, dropping fifty feet before coming to a hover. He cranked up the rear-facing propeller and guided the craft a short distance away before signaling Rita. She disengaged and likewise dropped, then hovered. Hammer Downe followed.

In a tight formation, they cleared the Cloud Cover and arced toward the large cigar box of a building opposite the runway. The three Fokker DVII fighters were in the air and busy dealing with Winchester and Preston, but the Nazi ground crew were still milling about. The wail of approaching auto-gyros drew their attention.

Justice counted nine. Several bolted for the hangar. Several more drew pistols and began firing at the descending Intrepid team.

Hammer executed a sharp left bank as Justice and Rita banked right. Downe opened up on the remaining ground crew with one of his Thompsons and the Nazis fled toward the hangar.

Justice and Rita landed hard on the roof of the cigar-box building, scattering gravel. They came to a teetering halt fifty feet from each other. Both cut power to their rotors, unstrapped, and retrieved their machine guns.

Downe circled the roof, providing cover fire.

Justice and Rita charged the access hatch, their machine guns slung over their shoulders.

Sky Hawk Winchester nosed the F4B upward in a vertical climb. Wind tore at his hair. His Clark Gable grin was at its fullest.

Guns Preston, facing downward, gripped the fuselage with salt-white knuckles. The force of the acceleration crushed him into his harness. "Holy smoke!" he bellowed.

"Hang on," Winchester called out. Neither man could hear the other over the gale.

Winchester flipped the F4B in a tight, inverted loop. The plane screamed.

The maneuver was fast. In short seconds, Winchester leveled off directly behind one of the pursuing Fokkers. At a deft motion of his thumbs, twin ribbons of .30-caliber rounds tore into the fins, rudder, and wings of the Nazi bi-plane.

At that same moment, Preston rotated the rear gun and lined his sights on the second Fokker before the Nazi pilot knew what was happening. Preston fired. The fuselage of the Fokker blew apart as if a grenade had exploded inside it.

Winchester barrel-rolled the F4B as the two Fokkers corkscrewed toward the Atlantic, trailing smoke and flaming debris.

The third Fokker burst through a cumulus formation to their rear, thirty degrees to their starboard, and slightly above them. Nazi bullets spat from its machine guns, ripping into the fabric of the F4B's wing tips.

The roof hatch was locked. Justice fired a three-round burst from his Thompson, splintering the frame. He jerked the hatch free and bounded down the ladder in rapid steps. Rita followed on his heels.

The ladder terminated in a dark passageway, damp and smelling of decay. Justice recognized the odor as the stench that spewed from the corpse he had encountered and shot on the Delaware beach the day before. It was milder and more dispersed, but the same stink, nevertheless. Rita gasped, covering her nose and mouth.

Justice ran down the passageway to where it ended at another larger and better lit corridor. He stopped, hugged the scratchy brick wall, and gingerly peered around the corner. Rita slid to a stop behind him.

Justice could see nothing to his left except more corridor. Naked incandescent light bulbs hung from the ceiling at regular intervals. He saw a series of wooden doors on both sides, and a heavy metal door at the far end. Above the door, an amber light flashed on and off.

Justice saw only a single door to his right. Judging by its construction, Justice surmised this was the exterior door that faced the air strip.

"Let's move," he whispered.

They stalked down the corridor, machine guns at the ready. The first door was unlocked. The room beyond it was nothing more than a utility closet. The next door was also unlocked. Rows of unmade and empty bunks and footlockers, many painted with Nazi swastikas, lined the walls.

The riveted metal door below the flashing amber light burst open with a screech of rusty hinges and a clang as it slammed into the corridor wall. A wave of stench blew out from the space past that door and in advance of a half dozen mottled corpses staggering toward them with dead, groping hands.

"Holy smoke, Hawk!" Preston bellowed. The trail of bullet holes along the corner of the upper wing perforated the fabric like Swiss cheese.

The Fokker slipped behind the F4B in a smooth arc. The Nazi pilot kept enough distance between them to prevent Winchester from executing the same maneuver that had doomed the other two Fokkers.

The Fokker fired. Winchester banked sharp. Preston opened up on the enemy plane.

The Fokker banked and rolled.

Winchester nosed the F4B into a steep, vertical dive. The Fokker followed, literally in the F4B's wake. Preston gripped the Browning, but couldn't fire at the Fokker without shredding the F4B's tail. The Fokker's machine guns spat at them.

The F4B drilled into a thick cloud layer. Winchester immediately pulled up on the stick and stood on the rudders. The Fokker rocketed past them. The Nazi pilot realized, too late, the cloud layer was actually the island's camouflage. The Fokker crashed nose-first into the rocky island and exploded in a fireball.

Winchester leveled off, banked, and pointed the F4B at the island's runway.

Colonel Rick Justice blew the head off the first zombie with a three-round burst. The corpse fell to the stone floor in a heap. Two more tripped over the cadaver and the remaining three angled around them in a stupor. Justice dispatched the trio with rapid bursts of the Thompson to their heads.

The other two untangled themselves and were mere feet from Justice when his gun jammed. The nearest zombie grasped Justice's throat with decaying fingers. The second corpse reached for Justice and he kicked it in the torso, sending it staggering back several feet.

A twelve-round burst from Rita's machine gun disintegrated its head and part of its shoulder. It dropped to the floor, oozing dark fluids and noxious odor.

Justice rammed the barrel of the Thompson up underneath the corpse's jaw. The thing loosened its grip and Justice peeled the fingers off his throat, then shoved the creature away from him. Rita finished it with a short burst.

Justice wasted no time on thanks. He pivoted and joined Rita at the last door. She shot the frame into splinters, and he shouldered it open.

The room was dark and hot. It stank, not so much of the odor of decomposition as the sharp and bitter stink of men living too closely for too long in unhygienic conditions. A single low-wattage light bulb cast a carrot glow over the shapes of the men huddled in a far corner. Their faces were drawn tight, their eyes peeled wide in fear.

"I'm Lieutenant Colonel Rick Justice, United States Army Air Corps. We're here to rescue you."

The even modulation of his voice and the smoothness of its timbre reached the men before his words did.

"T-thank God," said one. Others murmured and they tottered toward the two from Intrepid. Justice counted nine and did the math. Thirty-two taken. Four dead on

the coast. Six dead here. Nine alive here.

"Where are the other thirteen of you?" Justice asked.

"D-don't know," one said. "They would work on us. Then…then kill us. Then bring us back, but it wasn't us. Not anymore. Not anymore. They would throw some of the bodies into the ocean. The ones that didn't change right away. Then they'd c-come for more."

"But, why?" Rita asked.

"They're searching for a way to reuse dead soldiers," someone in the dim room told them.

"Where did they take you?" Justice asked. As one, they pointed to the room beyond the riveted metal door.

"Rita," Justice said evenly. "Get these men to the *Liberty*. The door in the wall of the other end of the corridor leads to the outside." He pulled his flare pistol from his waistband.

"Right, Rick." She took the flare pistol. "This way, boys," she said to the survivors, and led them away.

Justice unholstered his hand gun, ensured a round was in the chamber, and stepped around the pile of corpses, headless and now truly dead. He stepped through the riveted metal door and into the largest expanse in the building.

The chamber was crammed with queer-looking machinery and apparatus. Glaring white lighting radiated from long tubes recessed in the ceiling and protected by mesh. A crackling sound resounded in the room, like electricity snaking between open diodes. And the stench was pervasive.

Justice angled between machines toward the back where a pulsing amber glow bathed the grated ceiling. He heard excited voices ahead. Instructions being issued. Questions being asked. The voices—he counted six—spoke German.

Justice leaned close to a metal cabinet and peered around it. Three bodies were strapped to hospital gurneys. They lay motionless, their bloody shirts ripped open. Alongside each gurney, a duo of men draped in blood-stained surgical gowns, their mouths and noses covered by white surgical masks, worked over them. They injected the bodies with thick, pumpkin-colored fluid from fat syringes. They strapped electrodes to their foreheads and shot electric current through their dead brains. One by one, the dead men shuddered until they were self-animate.

Justice saw six more men strapped to gurneys farther back. These appeared alive; at least, their chests were in motion and their heads swayed from side to side. Mildly sedated, Justice surmised. That made nine. Where were the other four?

Two more gowned and masked men appeared from out of his line of sight and approached the six sedated prisoners. Both men carried heavy daggers, their serrated blades crusted in dark crimson. They hadn't even bothered to clean the weapons after their last use.

He could delay no longer. Justice bolted from his concealment, firing. His first two shots tore through the head of the first reanimated corpse as it was still climbing off the gurney. The gown-clad men scattered.

The second and third zombies thrashed off their gurneys and wobbled toward Justice, even as he shot them. His rounds were true, dispatching them both in short

seconds.

He heard the scraping behind him too late to react.

A pair of scabbed and festering arms encircled him. The growl in his ear was feral. The stench of decomposition choked him.

Justice cocked his head back into the creature's face. Its growl skipped. He did it again, even as he heard the other three scraping toward him.

A third time he ratcheted his head back, and this time Justice felt the corpse's nose splinter. Its growl intensified, but its grip loosened enough for Justice to free his right arm. He brought his .45 up, twisted his aim over his shoulder, and fired. The proximity of the explosion sent a stab of searing pain through his ears, as if a hot poker had been thrust into his head.

The corpse dropped to the cold floor. The other stepped over it. Justice backed up, his magazines empty.

A burp of automatic weapons fire from behind tore into the concrete wall next to him, blasting chalky shards in all directions. Justice dropped to a crouch as half-a-dozen Nazis burst into the chamber.

Nazis to his left. Zombies to his right.

Justice reached into the over-sized pockets of his khakis and pulled out a pair of hand grenades. He pulled the pins and lobbed one to each side. He dove for the gurneys and rolled underneath the nearest one, pulling the closest headless corpse along with him.

The grenades went off simultaneously in a deafening blast that shook the structure. Chalk and debris rained down from the high ceiling. Shrapnel ricocheted in all directions. The corpse Justice used as a shield took the full force of the blast. Justice, his head ringing afresh, his clothes tattered and bloody, was otherwise unscathed.

He pushed the corpse away and stood in the smoky confines of the chamber, then scampered over to the six remaining prisoners. They were alive.

"Holy smoke!" Preston said as he, Winchester, and Downe angled into the room, their Thompsons at the ready.

"Rick," Winchester called though the smoke.

"Over here, Hawk," Justice called back. "I've got survivors."

The three members of Intrepid stepped over the bodies and met up with Rick Justice.

"Rita has the others on board the *Liberty*," Downe reported. "Glasses is standing by to pick up the rest."

"Outstanding," Justice said. "Hammer, you and Guns get the rest of the prisoners to the *Liberty*. Hawk and I will lay the charges."

***

Less than fifteen minutes later, the last of the prisoners had been loaded into the cargo gondola. Sky Hawk Winchester and Rick Justice had planted explosives at key points in the chamber. Winchester had then retrieved the F4B and was circling overhead. Justice, Preston, and Downe had recovered the auto-gyros. Twenty minutes later, they were all on board the *Liberty* and watching through scopes as the explosives detonated and the structure of horror collapsed in on itself, taking with it its terrible secrets.

"So much for Case Gray," Wellington said.

"Maybe not," Winchester said. All eyes turned toward him.

"Why do you say that, Hawk?" Justice asked.

"After we had landed and were making our way to you, we saw another Fokker take off."

(Continued on page 121)

THE CASE FOR ERLE STANLEY GARDNER

AUTHOR OF "BLOODY BILL OBEYS"

Having your creations become better known then you are is a fate that has fallen to many authors. A perfect example is Erle Stanley Gardner (1889 – 1970), creator of Perry Mason who is making a comeback in an HBO original series.

Today's audiences most likely know of Perry Mason from re-runs of the 1950s tv series or the later tv-movies, both starring Raymond Burr. But they know nothing of his creator.

Certainly, they are probably unaware that Gardner wrote more than 80 Perry Mason novels and short stories from the 1930s to the 70s, which led to movies and radio shows predating the tv series.

Gardner was a practicing attorney who started to write on the side in the early 1920s, mainly for *Black Mask*, where he created a variety of series characters. He was their longest running author, eventually branching out to other magazines. His longest running series was Ed Jenkins with about 75 stories. He was the "Phantom Crook", a master of disguise who pitted cops against other crooks for personal gain.

Lester Leith is a close second at over 60 stories, mainly in *Detective Fiction Weekly*. Leith is a lawyer and "gentleman thief," who goes after thieves, swindlers and other low-life. He scams them out of their ill-gotten loot, giving it to charity (after deducting 20% for himself).

Gardner's other characters include Sidney Zoom, the Patent Leather Kid, and Paul Pry.

An interesting, if short lived character is Ken Corning. Lasting all of 6 stories in 1932 and 33, some see him as a model for Perry Mason as both are crusading lawyers who aren't afraid to get hands on in an investigation. Perry Mason showed up in 1933, but not in the pulps.

Gardner continued in the pulps into the 1940s, but focused more on his books, non-fiction, and occasional fiction pieces in the slick magazines (*Saturday Evening Post, Country Gentleman, Collier's,* etc.).

"Bloody Bill Obeys" (next page) appeared in the January 1925 issue of the *Chicago Ledger*, a weekly story paper put out by W.D. Boyce. It appeared under the alias of Charles M. Green, like much of Gardner's early work.

This is one of two Gardner stories published in the Ledger. It's surmised the story was rejected by *Black Mask* and other pulps. The story was purchased in 1924, but not published until 1925.

— *Michael R. Brown,*
  "The Pulp Super-Fan"

"Ah, yes, ladies and gentlemen, Mr. Silvey, Mr. William Silvey, a resident of your thriving little city, has consented to assist me."

Art: J. Brozik

BLOODY BILL OBEYS

BY

ERLE STANLEY

GARDNER

William Silvey, or "Bill" Silvey, as he preferred to be called, and known to more than half of the town of Colma as "Woozy Bill," sat in front of the fire hall whittling a pine stick. Before him passed the leading citizens of Colma, but they did not notice Bill.

Mike Kelley, the self-important chief of police—notice, for instance, the way he twirled his night stick. Bosh! How was he any better than Bill? But he wouldn't notice Bill; oh, no, not on your life! Bill was a "bum." Not one of the kind Kelley exactly dared to beat up and throw in the jail, but, nevertheless, in the social strata of Colma, a "bum."

Bill spat into the gutter and turned his eyes from the burly frame of the chief.

Into the center of his vision walked Judge Miller, striding along, his wife clinging proudly to his arm, showing by every detail of their bearing the social prestige which the pair claimed as their judicial prerogative.

Again Bill shifted his eyes and spat.

Judge Miller! Judge Miller indeed! And where would Judge Miller have been if it hadn't been for Bill's father. Judge Miller made Bill sick. Why Bill's own father had seen the potential development of the oil industry in Colma years before Judge Miller ever dreamed of it. Then when Bill's father died, the Judge, then a practicing attorney, had handled the estate. He had offered Bill a flat sum in cash money for Bill's interest in the property. Of course Bill had accepted—cash meant something in those days when saloons carried on their business as openly as ice cream counters.

Five years later they struck oil. Five years later—and Attorney Miller was Judge Miller, and William Silvey was "Woozy Bill," and a bum.

Meditatively Bill scanned the faces of the people walking past. Nearly all of them he knew, had known all his life. No one spoke to him, did not even turn their faces in his direction. Look at Lottie Vincent. Bill

---

Originally published in *Chicago Ledger*, 1925 January 3rd as by Charles M. Green

went to school with her. She had been his first sweetheart. Just after Bill's father died Lottie had been mighty sweet to Bill. That party at Cora Brown's for instance—how she had swayed close to him as they walked in the garden between dances. Her face kept turning up to his, and she had a trick of holding her face so that her profile caught the soft glint of the mellow moonlight. Oh, yes, that red rose she held—Bill had nearly forgotten that. She held it to her lips, gently kissed the warm, red petals, then carelessly rubbed it against Bill's cheek.

How she had struggled when Bill clasped her to him. Not hard enough to get away, of course, but hard enough so that Bill had to grasp her tightly. Then suddenly she had yielded. Her soft body grew limp in his arms as she raised her face to his and let his hot lips take their fill of that rosebud mouth.

Now Lottie Vincent, not quite as young as she used to be, but still dainty, sweet, feminine, walked past the firehouse without even noticing the figure on the bench, although her gaze wandered over it impersonally. That was the hard part. She had made no conscious effort to avoid meeting his eyes. She had forgotten, had ceased to think of him, did not even remember him as a person she had ever known.

Bill was a bum.

Half a block down the street the doors of the "opera house" were ablaze with light. The entrance was crowded with people who were gathering to hear Morton "The Mystic." Elaborate press notices had preceded the advent of the "Great Psychic;" flaming posters showing the great Morton with the devil, himself, looking over the

shoulder of the magician, had been pasted on every fence, on the side of every barn. It was a great night in Colma.

The crowd parading past the firehouse thinned out; those who did come were hurrying rapidly along the street, intent on arriving before the first act of the great exhibition of "magic, psychology, telepathy and hypnotism" should commence.

The huge clock on the courthouse boomed one deep stroke. Half past eight. Still Bill sat on the bench before the firehouse, whittling. What else was there for him to do? When Judge Miller had seen how Bill's money was going, he had persuaded Bill to allow him to put the last payment in a "spendthrift trust." In a weak moment Bill had consented. Now he could count on drawing fifty dollars every month—and nothing more. It kept Bill clothed after a fashion, gave him a place to sleep, and a little food and tobacco. Bill did not work.

Occasionally he thought of the ten thousand dollars "tied up" in the spendthrift trust and he hated Judge Miller with a bitter hatred. Bill could never touch that ten thousand dollars; but always, as long as he should live, he received fifty dollars on the first day of each and every month.

Bill yawned, stretched his arms, put away his knife and arose…. Nothing to do…. He entered the firehouse. The group of firemen ceased their conversation and looked at him. Bill tried to join in the talk. He was lonesome, craved companionship; but the firemen did not open their little circle.

Bill made a remark on the weather, spoke of the show. No one answered. "Swede" Johnson, the big, broad-shouldered, burly chief of the fire crew spoke, slowly and impressively.

"Bill, the boys don't object to your hanging around on the benches outside; but this is sort of a private club in here, and—"

He paused significantly.

Bill spat, turned and walked out.

For ten or fifteen minutes he hung around the entrance of the opera house. It was a warm night, and the doors were open. Bill could hear the lecturer within talking about "secondary personalities."

Something stirred within Bill's mind.

It was not as if Bill had never acquired an education. He had been in the second year of college when his father had died.

Vague recollections of college lectures—hitherto forgotten terms, the hazy collections of memory's storehouse, intruded upon his conscious mind. He edged toward the doorway.

The lecturer continued:

"The only danger of hypnotism—if indulged in by amateurs—is the possible development of a secondary personality in the subject. Such cases are frequent and well authenticated. A mild-mannered man may become 'possessed' of a secondary personality and become a bloodthirsty outlaw. A tried and trusted citizen may become a thief. A meek, refined, modest, young lady of retiring disposition may become a forward adventuress—a shoplifter—a pickpocket. I mention these dangers in order that you may be warned against allowing any person to repeatedly hypnotize you; and also to explain why I carry no one with me who acts as a professional subject. There is almost no danger in a case of iso-lated hypnotism now and then, and for that reason I always choose my subjects from the audience.

"Is there some person who will step forward and assist me in demonstrating the phenomena of hypnotism? I ask for volunteers, men who are well known and above reproach in the community."

In the pause there came the rustle of whispers, the crinkle of programs....

No one stepped forward.

Bill turned to the street, spat upon the sidewalk, and pushed his way into the door of the theater.

"Bah!" he muttered to himself. "I know more about psychology than this bird ever saw; I've forgotten more about hypnotism than he ever knew. I'll just show him up good and plenty."

A uniformed attendant barred his way, hand outstretched for a ticket. Then, seeing Bill was on his way toward the platform, stepped back, took Bill's arm and escorted him down the aisle.

Morton, "The Mystic," smiled ingratiatingly as Bill stepped upon the stage.

"The name, please?"

"William Silvey."

"Ah, yes, ladies and gentlemen, Mr. Silvey, Mr. William Silvey, a resident of your thriving little city has consented to assist me.

"Now, Mr. Silvey, if you will please look directly into my eyes, make no conscious effort at thinking, but relax, just let yourself go; think of rest, sleep—quiet—complete rest.

"No, pardon me, Mr. Silvey. You are resisting me, fighting against the influence.... Now just stand quiet. Count slowly

"No, pardon me, Mr. Silvey. You are resisting me, fighting against the influence .... You're getting just a little drowsy .... Your lids are getting heavy, you breathe deeper and slower, your muscles are relaxing—"

to one hundred in your mind. Concentrate on the counting.... Now, that's better. You're getting just a little drowsy.... The figures come to your mind a little slower, your lids are getting heavy, you breathe deeper and slower, your muscles are relaxing—"

Bill was determined to show this man up. To give him a fair chance, but to show him up just the same. Almost he gave the man too fair a chance. Suddenly, as he counted, he felt a great weight of darkness descending on his brain. Almost too late he realized he was slipping; for what seemed an age his consciousness battled with the enveloping cloud of blackness. Sometimes the struggle seemed hardly worthwhile. It would be so delightful to slip quietly down the stream of drowsiness.... But no! He struggled...and then, suddenly, he shook off the deadening stupor. He opened his eyes.

In that moment he realized that he had met the hypnotist in a battle of brains and had emerged victor. The crisis was past. Merton the Mystic couldn't hypnotize Bill Silvey!

A new pride shot through his mind; a new energy seemed to course through his nerves. Bill the bum! Indeed! He'd show 'em.

Striding from the stage, a new vigor in his gait, he noticed with satisfaction the looks of respect which were flashed at

him by the audience. He seemed to have regained his old-time pride and independence—to have resumed his former social position—only they needed to be shown. It was up to Bill Silvey to show 'em.

Without a word to anyone he left the theater. As he stepped to the sidewalk and noticed the place where he had spat upon the concrete a few minutes before, he smiled—a grim, deadly smile.

What a change had taken place within him since he had entered the theater! He was a different man. Something had awakened within him.

"I'll show 'em," he muttered to himself.

Then, to his surprise, and seeming to be the utterance of some personality within his own brain, there sounded a voice:

"You've been insulted within the past half hour. Go get that man. Show him first."

A capital idea. Rushing down the street he entered the firehouse. The same group was there engaged in the same endless discussion—politics, prohibition, peace— always gabbling, always wrangling; the discussion which waged always, interminable, monotonous, never getting anywhere.

Bill had become a man of action. How he hated this perpetual talkfest, this small-town babble, babble, babble!

He walked up to "Swede" Johnson, the burly fire chief, amateur boxer, wrestler, town bully.

Johnson stepped forward. Having told Bill to keep out, his face darkened when he saw the unwelcome visitor again entering the firehall.

Bill started to say something, to explain to "Swede" that a new Bill Silvey stood before him; but again that voice took a hand.

"What's the use talking? Hit him! Pound him to pieces—show him who's who."

Bill instantly recognized the logic of the remark. He braced his right foot behind him, twisted slightly from the hips and brought forward his right fist in a terrific swing.

With the instinctive motion of a trained boxer, Johnson, surprised though he was, sidestepped and threw up his arm.

Too late! With a savage speed and strength which Bill had never known himself to possess he crashed the blow squarely on Johnson's jaw.

Bill felt the crunching impact, felt his muscles tense with the sudden crash of the blow, and in that instant lowered his shoulder, thrust forward his body, and threw his entire weight into a quick shoulder-snap— the most deadly blow of the prize ring.

A fraction of a split-second Johnson stood, braced against the force of the blow, a fighting machine, seeking to keep his feet, to return the blow he had received. Then his head snapped back, the neck muscles relaxed and a dull "snap" sounded through the firehouse.

The huge frame, collapsed and slumped to the floor, the neck strangely twisted.

"My God! The man's dead," exclaimed one of the firemen, as he bent over the body of his fallen chief.

Taking advantage of the confusion, Bill walked out. Instinctively he felt that he was a fugitive from justice. A lot he cared. "Woozy Bill," eh? They'd get a new name for him before this night's work was over.

They'd be looking for him. He'd have to find some place to hide for a while. All right, what was the matter with the court-house? They'd never think of looking for him there.

Quickly he walked down the street until he came to the Court House Square. The huge, dark pile of the building loomed before him.

Now let's see. The Justice's office was downstairs and there was a window which would probably be open. He could crawl in that. The sheriff's office was right above, but it wouldn't do to stay there; they'd be organizing a posse. He'd better step in there and get a gun, though. He'd need some weapon before the night was out.

Before the night was out? Yes. It was going to be some night. The town had wronged Bill, and he intended to see that the town paid for it, and tonight was going to see a lot of old scores settled.

He found the window open as he expected; nor did he find any difficulty in getting to the office of the sheriff. But he did find that all the weapons were locked behind the massive door of the gun room. Only a glass case, hanging on the wall contained the weapons with which past crimes had been committed. These deadly implements all had a history.

Bill opened the door of the cabinet. The revolvers had no shells. Never mind. A big dirk, glinting wicked and ominous in the dim light which came from the street-light on the corner, gave him a feeling of security.

There was a tag on it. "People vs. Smith, (people's exhibit 'A')." Bill didn't remember the details of the crime for which Smith had been hung; but he did remember something of the general circumstances, the awful slaughter which Smith had committed with this long-bladed dirk. "Bloody" Smith they had called him. Well, before another sunrise they'd be calling him "Bloody Bill."

He tiptoed back to the office of the Justice of the Peace, sat in the cushioned chair on the little platform, and put his feet on the Justice's desk—waiting.

Soon there came the roar of automobiles, racing down the street. Footsteps rushed up the wooden stairs of the courthouse to the sheriff's office. He could hear the metallic slam of breech locks as sawed off shotguns were loaded, then the sounds died away. From farther down the street he heard the shriek of the siren on the county police car as it swept down the road.

Sitting there in the warm darkness, his feet on the desk of justice, occupying the chair in much the same manner as the Justice of the Peace whiled away the spare time, Bill grinned to himself.

Subconsciously he knew what he was going to do; but it was not until the clock above boomed the hour of midnight that he really faced the issue. Then the inner voice again issued its imperative summons to his mind.

"Midnight! Now for Judge Miller. After that … Lottie Vincent … then, and until dawn, as many as you can get."

Slinking down the shadows, prowling through alleys and back yards, Bill approached the magnificent residence of Judge Miller, the residence paid for with money derived from the property Bill's father had willed to his favorite son.

The back window was unlocked. Slowly Bill pried it open and stepped inside. At first the warm, velvety darkness inside bothered him a little; but only at first; Bill remembered that he was to work silently and in utter blackness. No flashlight for bloody Bill Silvey.

At almost that instant his eyes seemed to dilate, a peculiar relaxation of the pupil; and he heard a voice which he had come to recognize as that of the secondary personality saying: "Now you can see in the dark, just as a sleepwalker can walk with eyes closed. Judge Miller sleeps in the front bedroom on the second floor."

Silently as a cat Bill tiptoed through the house. He heard the tick-tock of the clock in the hall, the occasional creak of a floorboard. Aside from this there was the silence of midnight. Keeping close to the edge of the stairs so as to eliminate as much of the creaking as possible, Bill made his noiseless way to the upper hall.

It was intensely black up here, but Bill had acquired some means of stretching the iris of his eyes so as to enlarge the pupil. Even so, it was all he could do to make out the vague outlines of the room.

Slowly, silently, he turned the knob of the door at the extreme southern end of the hall and slipped into the room. He could hear the rhythmic breathing of the sleeper within. Cautiously, his hand clutching the deadly dagger, Bill sneaked forward.

A board creaked. The breathing of the man on the bed suddenly stopped. Intuitively Bill knew that he had awakened. Somehow in the electric atmosphere of that room, charged with his thoughts of murder, he sensed that Judge Miller knew he was not alone in the room, realized that somewhere within the darkest cold, deliberate murder stalked.

Bill smiled. He preferred it that way.

The bedsprings creaked as the Judge sat up.

Bill's hand touched the corner of the bed as he groped along the covers. The coarse skin on his hand made the faintest sound, an almost inaudible rasping as his hand moved along the linen.

The Judge heard the sound. Curiously, hardly able to believe that the warning given by his senses was correct, Judge Miller stretched forth his hand.

There in the dark, without warning, flesh touched flesh. The hand of the Judge cold and damp with fear. The hand of the murderer clutching the handle of the wicked knife.

A piercing scream rang out as Judge Miller attempted to leap from the hampering bed clothes. He never had the chance to struggle for his life. Bill plunged the knife, plunged it squarely into the scrawny chest of his victim — felt the point grate upon a rib, slip off and slide up to the hilt in the soft flesh — Warm blood spurted over his wrist as he withdrew the blade.

A single choked cry of surprise and consternation mingled with the death rattle in the throat of his victim as the body slumped to the floor.

Wiping the blade on the coverlet, Bill slipped noiselessly toward the door.

He heard a call from an adjoining room. Judge Miller's wife asked if everything was all right. Receiving no answer, she arose and Bill could hear her bare feet padding on the boards as she came down the hall.

Silently Bill drew himself up against the wall, knife poised, ready, an evil grin distorting his face.

"No, don't kill her," came the commanding voice in his ear.

Bill was disappointed. He sought to strike as the figure came closer; but he found he could not disobey the instructions of that voice. It had always been right so far, and he could not disregard its commands now.

Mrs. Miller slipped past him, so close that Bill could hear the beating of her heart. Almost the fold of her kimono brushed against Bill's clothes. Then she had passed and entered the Judge's bedroom.

"Why," she cried, "the floor's all sticky and wet! What's the matter?" A light flashed. A shriek echoed through the house.

"Blood, blood, blood!" she yelled.

Bill realized he had no time to waste.

He hurried from the house, departing silently by the front door. Already lights were flashing in adjoining houses. Bill knew that the police car would be on the scene in a few moments.

"Wait in the shadow of the hedge," counseled the voice.

With unhesitating obedience, Bill stepped within the deep shadows of the hedge. Soon an automobile skidded around the corner, and ground to a stop before the house. In the dim half-light Bill recognized the form of Chief of Police Johnson, as he left the automobile and hurried through the gate, his flashlight throwing a pencil of white light before him. Bill watched until the chief had rushed up the steps, and entered the front door of Judge Miller's house.

A neighbor cut across the lawn and hurried after the officer. In the distance Bill heard for the second time that night the shriek of the siren on the big armored car of the sheriff's office.

"Now," said the voice, "get in the chief's car and drive down the river road."

Quickly Bill rushed out from the hedge, entered the roadster, threw in the clutch and swept off down the street, as he did so the sheriff's car screamed around the corner.

Bill used his head start for all there was in it. He was swishing around the curves on the creek road when the headlights of the sheriff's car commenced to dance along the road behind him.

"Faster, faster, open the throttle, advance the spark," instructed the voice.

Automatically Bill threw the controls wide open and the little car thundered along the road, gathering speed on the gentle hills, topping them with a leap, and swooping down the other side, swaying and lurching, seeming to skim over the road.

Behind, he could hear the whine of the siren. Then there came a flash, the spatter of a bullet on the pavement near his car, followed by the droning whine of the lead as it ricocheted off into space.

The roadster skidded around a sharp turn, swinging almost broadside on the road, the rubber whining and shrieking as the tortured tire slid along the concrete surface. Roaring through the night the automobile shot up the incline which lay around the curve. Once more Bill heard the voice.

"Turn the car at the summit, put out the lights, head it back down the grade, put it in neutral and let it slam into the sheriff's car on the turn."

Acting with a speed and precision which Bill never knew he possessed, he slowed the car at the summit of the little grade, turned it around and whipped a string from his pocket. Heading the machine straight down the hill, he tied the steering wheel, put out the lights, kicked out the clutch, put the gears in neutral and stepped from the running board as the car gathered momentum.

For a few moments Bill watched it slipping swiftly away in the dark, then it was swallowed up in the night.

A few moments later, the sheriff's car lurched around the curve, and began roaring up the grade. As the lights settled down upon the road there loomed for a fraction of a second against the glare of the lights the huge bulk of the roadster. Then there came a terrific crash. The lights of the pursuing car went out. There came a wild scream, the grinding smash of wreckage piling up—then silence.

"There are pursuers coming down the road from the other direction. They've telephoned the office of the sheriff at Cold Springs," said the voice. "You'll have to swim the river and take to the woods."

With that unhesitating obedience which had characterized his conduct throughout the night, Bill scrambled and slipped down

(Continued on page 121)

MONA'S BACK

BY MICHAEL A. WEXLER

The gore didn't bother me.

I'd seen worse and done to better people than Meyer Hoffman.

The old German lay face up, framed by dusty moonlight seeping into the empty apartment. Shirt ripped open, hands and feet bound and a sock stuffed in his mouth like a trumpet mute. I counted an even dozen knife wounds dried red, brown and purple. Even his goatee was blood soaked.

Footsteps sounded in the hall. I backed quickly into the shadows behind the open door ahead of a flashlight sweeping across the threshold. It circled the room, a search beacon that fixed on the dead *fence* with a grunt of surprise. The light moved forward and with it the glint of a gun barrel. I waited, tensing behind a year of drink and personal decay. But when the intruder's back came square to me, I pulled it together.

The intruder stiffened as he felt my .45 poking his ribs.

"Keep the light on and drop the gun, unless you want to make it two corpses in

Those damn disks had enough dirt to retire every crime boss in town; Now Mona was back and they all wanted her dead.

one room."

Standing in the dark, issuing threats over the bloody remains of a dead mobster, you expect a reaction. You steel yourself for something cagey or something stupid. I'd buy mad, scared or even crazy ... anything but an amused laugh.

"You aren't really going to shoot me, are you Jack?"

The best I could manage was a surprised, "Harry?"

"Yeah, is there a light in here?"

Reaching overhead, I pulled the chain hanging from a single, naked bulb in the ceiling. I wasn't worried Detective Sergeant Harry Lima would shoot me — arrest me, maybe, if he wanted to press the issue, but not shoot me.

"Somebody sure took their time making the German talk," Harry noted nonchalantly, not yet facing me.

"Judging by the wet and the stink," I returned, "I'd say he's been dead less than an hour."

Harry turned. He looked as I remembered him, hard, grey, with a hooked nose and piercing eyes. He gave me the professional once over.

"You look surprisingly healthy ... for a rummy."

"Thanks," I returned bitterly, knowing I deserved the slap.

Last time Harry and I met up, I'd been leaning against the back wall of a shoddy barroom, knuckles bloodied and life in shambles. He'd given me a speech about self- respect and I'd cursed his ass and stormed out looking for the next drink, the next fight. I'd been that way almost a year and he was trying to figure the change — Jack Darwin in a pressed suit and a clean shave. Knowing the way cops figure things, sobering up takes cause; he was digging for the motive. I gave him the long and short of it in two words.

"Mona's back."

Harry walked over to the window, forced it open and pulled in a breath of fresh air. The night was quiet. The streetlights lining the old Bronx neighborhood standing sentinel over the sleeping innocents.

"Mona Lewis."

He said it as if swallowing poison, poison drawn from the same simmering well of hate entrapping me. That name, that woman, that wall, sprung up between best

MICHAEL A. WEXLER: "I was born and raised in Philadelphia, and had an exciting and enriching musical youth working with such personalities as Jimi Hendrix, Ike and Tina Turner, Chuck Berry and others. I began putting my creative juices to work as a part-time ghostwriter and editor, eventually settling into a career as a graphic designer. I continued writing novels and short stories in the Pulp Detective and Heroic Fantasy genre as my hobby, though never overly pursued publication. Today, I live in DeKalb, Illinois as a successful consultant to credit unions developing long-term growth strategies and marketing solutions for today's competitive marketplace. Success (age) and a decent 401k has given me the time to go back to my first love, writing."

friends. Yeah, we had been that way a long time before Mona, only I hadn't come up here to reminisce.

"Why did you come up here Jack?" Harry demanded as though I had shouted my thoughts through a megaphone. "How does that lying little bitch tie-up with someone dissecting of Meyer Hoffman? And Jack, do us both a favor. Make it good."

"Not much of a hello, Harry."

"You made your bed, pal. I'm way past sympathy with you. If you don't want a fast and furious with the DA then you talk to me, now."

I nodded as both Harry and I finally got around to holstering our .45s. It was nice of the Sergeant not to ask if my license was current.

"She was coming out of Hoffman's store. I eat at old Gansky's across the street a lot. He remembers how things were and discounts my bill."

"You talk to her?"

I shook my head.

"My guts were still in a bottle. I pissed my pants and went home to change drawers and drown myself. Only the longer I thought on it the less I drank. I wasn't thirsty anymore, just hungry."

He looked me up and down, looking for the motivation. "Revenge Jack, that what turned the trick?"

The scar under my chin, where a punk's knife had shaved a little too close, flamed red with the truth. Harry had seen that give-away before. Only in his book, it took more than a shower and a suit to call a man sober and it took more than words to make him trustworthy.

I could have told him how I still shook at night, that I wasn't the first drunk to use payback to take the bitters out of the booze. I could have mentioned the balls it took to come here knowing I was rusty, out of step and probably going in over my head. I could have but didn't. I didn't need that with Harry.

"OK, Jack, you took a cold shower and then what?"

"I half confided in old Gansky and he signed me on as a bus boy so I could watch the German's shop. No pay but I got to keep the tips."

"How long?"

"Nine days before she showed again. In the interim, the German had three visits from Lenny Brasno."

That got a reaction. "Hell, Lenny the Leech! What I wouldn't give … "

Harry choked the name up from that dark place every cop keeps his worst night-mares. He looked at the body again. "Yeah, it works for me. Hard to believe a woman could do that to somebody but they sure could cause it to happen." His eyes shot to mine. "So, nine days and Mona shows again and …

"She visits maybe five minutes, cab waiting. From Hoffman's it's directly to the airport and a flight to New Orleans."

"You follow her?"

"Follow her? Hell, I didn't have bus fare to Jersey."

"You said you were getting tips." Harry said it evenly, no smile. "So, you kept on Hoffman knowing only those stolen jewels could have brought Mona Lewis back to town and only those jewels could add up to Meyer Hoffman and Lenny Brasno."

I nodded, adding quickly, "Your turn

Harry. How'd you happen to show up here?"

Now he smiled. "You got sloppy Jack. Stoolies like to get paid not slapped around."

"Benny Kolpin," I growled. "I was too broke to pay him. Hell, he owed me anyway."

"It wasn't how he figured it. I got a call you were back from the dead and asking around about Meyer Hoffman."

"And Mona?"

"*Her* name never came up." The ice thawed just a little. "Christ Jack, why didn't you call me?"

"Oh, Hell, you know the answer to that one."

Of course he did. Harry just wasn't in a saying mood. City Hall didn't take to meddling PI's, even sober and reliable ones. Forget about one crawling back from the dead. Throw in a scent of vigilante justice and that would clinch it for the DA. When the news Mona was back and Hoffman was dead reached the papers he would smile all nice, call in a steno, spring for coffee and a bagel and then lock me up on suspicion of murder. That would leave Harry to go the distance alone. It wouldn't be about the applause because Harry didn't work that way. It would be about the rules.

Rules that said Detective Sergeant Harry Lima couldn't let me just go out, walk up to Mona Lewis, put a gun in her mouth, and pull the trigger. Sure, he'd taken it on the chin over her double-crossing disappearing act too. It was a hurt that went deep and kept him up at night but that didn't add up enough for him to cross the line departmental rules drew in the sand. Not

yet it didn't.

"OK, Jack, wherever the hell you thought you were going with this, it ends here. Mona is one thing, murder is another."

"Hoffman's or hers?"

"Either damn it, you know the drill. I write my report and as sure as the Yankees spend money, the press grabs it and splashes it across tomorrow's papers in capital letters. Mona's back! Meyer Hoffman killed and Jack Darwin held for questioning."

"How about *wanted for questioning*?"

His eyes flashed. "I won't carry your water, Jack."

"I'm not asking you to," I responded angrily. "Somehow the Leech got wind Mona was back and she'd run to Hoffman to fence those jewels. The Leech had the German grabbed and brought here and, well, no need to elaborate. He talked."

Harry thought it through. "Think he has the jewels already?"

"No. There's something else going on or Mona wouldn't still be out there. Meyer Hoffman's not the only fence in the world. There was no need for her to risk coming back to town just to deal with him unless …"

"Ah hell," Harry spit. "Are you suggesting Mona plans financing a takedown of Brasno down?"

"She has the disks. What she needed was muscle and Hoffman was just connected enough to make it happen. Give me twenty-four hours, Harry."

"This isn't a movie, Jack. What the hell do you take me for anyway?"

"A friend," I answered quietly.

I was reaching out and Harry hadn't expected that. He understood Mona had been my client, my lover and my Waterloo. But her game had cut him down a few pegs as well. He might still make Captain but the path was tenfold harder. Which is why, while he could never condone what I'd done to myself, Harry understood why I'd done it. Why I crawled into that bottle and what it would take to climb out … all the way out.

"The rules say I have to write a report," he said with a slow smile. "But I guess they don't say how soon. OK Jack, you have twenty-four hours before I file my report that you were seen leaving the building."

Mona Lewis had walked into my office nearly a year ago begging for protection from her boyfriend, Artie Levin. He was what the street called a soft-song man, a pretty boy running confidence games and mostly on lonely old ladies. He worked for Lenny the Leech Brasno, the big noise nobody could quiet.

She laid it on thick how Artie had drunkenly spilled the dope on a million-dollar heist Lenny had worked out, gems coming into Tiffany and Company from some European estate. He had it all on the record, and a lot more, a couple of disks that held the financial records of Lenny Brasno and half a dozen under lieutenants. He was using possession of the disks as blackmail for the jewels. When he sobered up, he got hot about it, threatening Mona to keep her mouth shut, threats that got physical.

She wanted out; and from the moment I laid eyes on her, I wanted in.

I took the case downtown knowing Harry and the DA had been working with the Feds for two years on Brasno. When Mona spilled what she had, the DA had champagne corks ready to pop. Suddenly, he had Lenny Brasno gutted and hung out to dry if he had the jewels and the disks. That was the play and Mona had sold it all the way around.

For two weeks, I played the white knight, watching Artie, sheltering Mona. With her testimony, the Feds had no trouble securing warrants. Everything fell into place. Only when we went crashing through Artie Levin's apartment door for the grand finale, all we found was blood and dust.

Levin provided the blood, Mona the dust.

She had it all; we had nothing.

Sure, the DA dragged Brasno in and tried to make a case but he was swatting flies with a piece of string and everybody knew it.

Then came the blame game, with accusations flying like leaves under a blower. The always politically ambitious DA made me the fall guy, and the papers ate it up. It was sharks after chum. They revoked my license pending some investigation that never came off and I dove into a bottle, drained my savings and waited for the word Mona was dead.

Europe, Russia or the goddamn Himalayas, Brasno would find her. Nobody double-crossed Lenny the Leech and lived.

Yeah, she was good as dead and for nothing, too. Of what use were those disks to a woman on the lam and no way could she ever fence that load. That would take connections she didn't have and couldn't make because it would all flow right back to Lenny Brasno.

Except for the German; he was just

ambitious enough to buck Brasno for a million-dollar split seventy-five twenty-five in his favor; a split that also removed Brasno as competition. Yeah, greed was the one emotion bigger than fear in the heart of Meyer Hoffman. And, in his heart had been were that final knife thrust had gone.

So Mona chanced coming back to town … but why, really. Something in the back of my aching head told me there had to be something bigger than the money for Mona to risk getting within arm's reach of Lenny Brasno. But what was it?

What could be bigger than a million dollars?

***

Benny Kolpin was an arranger. For a price, he could arrange most anything.

I'd tumbled onto Hoffman's death scene by tailing Meyer to a meeting with Benny and when it broke up, I slid out of the shadows and shoved the protesting fat man into a dark alley. It took some coaxing but the pressure of my hands around his neck helped Benny remember who I'd been and how far I'd go to be that bastard again. He cracked like an old pot.

Benny fixed it for Hoffman to hire out of town muscle. The meet was set for the vacated apartment of Milo Stepponovitch, who the state had relocated up the Hudson for twenty years. Mona had baggage and Hoffman was hiring insurance. He should have saved his money. I'd have bet a hundred I didn't have that Benny sold the German out to Lenny Brasno for ten times what Hoffman paid or promised to pay.

Brasno hadn't dragged Hoffman up to that room. Benny planted him there.

Just for the hell of it, I left Benny in need of a dentist. Stupid move as it was surely that bit of self-indulgence that had him tipping Harry to the apartment even as he'd tipped Brasno. Why he didn't run to Brasno instead of the cops I chalked up to the primary rule of a good snitch. Never know too much, like who murdered who and why. You become dispensable.

Spread through the Bronx you could find a dozen corners where the paths of people like Lenny Brasno and Mona Lewis converged. My plan was to *converge* a few heads together until I got some juice.

Cruising gin joints and saloons without imbibing should have come hard. It came easy. No urges, no detours, no loss of purpose. I slowly realized I had never been a real drunk at all but a lame ass stooge who couldn't get over being duped and dumped. I smiled at the irony. It was Mona Lewis pushed me over the edge. It was Mona Lewis dragging me back.

Not having been around much except when lathered, it was no surprise I drew a few stares stepping into Falatico's Italian eatery all bright eyed and bushy tailed, spit shine on my shoes and a tight smile on my lips. I wasn't as big as before but I was harder, the kind of crust that grows on a man over twelve months nursing hate.

The hood at the door eyed me but didn't know me. I walked in and, in the back corner, spotted what I was after. Six jokers huddled at their perennially reserved table holding court over dirty dishes and a bottle of Chianti.

These men knew me, and my resurrection had eyes opening fast as a switchblade. Two had names. One was Darius Edwards, attorney-at-law. How did the Supreme Court let this one get away? Edwards had looks, presence, and more than enough brains to go around. As fast as cops put his crowd in jail, he got them out. He rarely lost and never got his own due for the shyster practice he ran.

The other was Jimmy Briganti. Jimmy Bones, as people in the neighborhood knew him, had separated himself from the run-of-the-mill gunsmith via an unhealthy bend for the nasty. His hallmark feature were large, wide spread eyes that, like the snake he resembled, could see you approach from all angles, seemingly without turning his head. He could also send a message without speaking; but then so could I.

I stopped at the table and watched Jimmy's eyes roll inward and up.

"Jack Darwin," he wheezed. Too much smoke and not enough fresh air had left his lungs black as his personality. He looked around at his boys and flashed a gold tooth. "Least you look like Jack Darwin."

There was some snickering at my expense. I let it go.

"What the hell you want around here?"

"Mona's back."

There was no pretext of being amused. "That broad, no way she shows her face around here, no way and no how. Lenny would have her head on a platter."

I grinned so hard that scar across my chin stretched until it glowed white.

"Drop it Jimmy, I found Hoffman. So have the cops."

I expected a denial; there wasn't one. Instead, he exchanged quick looks with Edwards who nodded almost imperceptibly. Jimmy got to his feet, a couple of his oversized goons following. Like Harry, Jimmy was staring me down, connecting the dots from past to present. I waited and let the little hood drink in the whole picture, watching the deep flush rise from his neck to his cheeks. At length, he hissed hard in my ears because his bad lungs kept him from yelling.

"You listen, Darwin. You got balls to come here and ride me about that dame. We've been letting things slide with you because there really aren't any bragging rights whacking a wino. But make trouble and that pass goes away, fast. You get my drift?"

"I get your breath and it stinks. As for letting things slide, I'm the one that let things slide Jimmy and way too long. So, understand this. Whether you realize it or not you and Lenny now have two big problems. Mona's one, I'm the other."

"That so?"

"Yeah, that's so. A year ago, I had your boss dead to rights. Mona blew it sky high, sure, and she broke me doing it but she wasn't any less subtle about screwing Lenny, was she? So, let's not play games. She's back; Hoffman is dead; so one of two things is happening. She's a zillion miles away from here and still running or she's trying to parlay another sucker to take up the slack. Lenny wants her bad, but I promise you I'll find her first, and when I do, I'm going to make her crap all over your organization; and this time it's gonna stick!"

Jimmy let those serpent eyes narrow to heated fissures. "You sound real tough

Darwin only I'll lay odds if you do find Mona first, she'll just rub your tummy and make you roll over. Meow!"

The gang behind him snickered. My anger built fast but I put a lid on it. That or be up to my ass in hoods and the guest of honor at a coroner's inquest.

"I'm done playing the sap. See you around, Jimmy."

I turned to go showing my back and my contempt. Nobody moved. Still, there was something disquieting in the silence. Something incongruent I couldn't make work against the vicious personalities in my rear-view mirror. Mirror, sure, that was it. In the bar mirror to my left I saw Jimmy smiling. He nodded ever so slightly and the hood working the front door slipped into my path flexing his muscles.

How much had I come back? Was I really a man again or just a wishful old drunk play-acting at respectability? In the next seconds, I found out. I ducked a right hand swinging up from the guy's belt buckle and grabbed up a wire breadbasket from a table. I pushed the chain-like meshing in the punk's face and while he fumbled, I rumbled. The side of my hand curled hard into his Adam apple and I followed that with a fist that went right through the damn basket and broke his nose.

The fight over, Jimmy's boy went to his knees spitting vomit that worked its way into the red spittle dripping from his nose. Now they all started to move and my illegal .45 came out and wagged its tail. Jimmy wasn't thinking of backing off but Edwards took charge, quietly ordering the pack to heel while whispering into Jimmy's ear; words of wisdom no doubt? I cut loose

with the best belly laugh I'd had in a very long time.

"Hey Jimmy, ever see a guy get it in the breadbasket before? Tell Lenny I'll be in touch."

The storm brewed in Jersey then floated across the Hudson to drop a pall over the city. People quickened their steps to beat it home or swam into the nearest watering hole to ride it out. Me, I embraced it. The wildness too long missing from my life energized me, made me feel vital and alive.

The rain came and I walked right down the middle of Broadway wrapped in a watery cocoon and grinning. No one could touch me. The stench of the bottle, the shame of a lost year, it bled off me in cascading sheets and washed into the sewers, so too the chill of withdrawal.

I took a head count of an old circle freshly visited, Harry Lima and Mona Lewis, Jimmy Bones and Lenny Brasno.

"Give an old dog a familiar scent and he's off to the woodpile without thinking."

Right about now, Jimmy Bones was thinking about the deliberate hint I'd dropped. That Mona was working the streets for the German's replacement. He was taking his own headcount. There were only two candidates. Al Decker, a local small timer who'd always operated in the shadow of the high rolling Brasno and the Blank brothers, an uptown operation operating on a truce of convenience, predicated on staying clear of each other's turf.

Maybe they could be convinced to violate the peace if they thought they could win the war.

I followed that with a fist that went right through the damn basket and broke his nose.

I stopped at a pay phone and dialed Harry.

"I assume you've got men on all the exits out of town."

"The blanket is out. Especially on anything going to Mardi Gras."

"I had a chat with Jimmy Bones."

"Who got killed?"

"No one, yet, Darius was there and kept Jimmy sensible for the moment. I'll bet another year of my life that bastard did Hoffman himself."

"No takers here."

"Harry, I played a little gimmick with Jimmy. You might want to keep an eye on Al Decker and —"

"The Blank Brothers?" There was a pause and a laugh. "You were the one who fell asleep for a year, not me. Call when you got something important. And, Jack …?"

"Yeah?"

"Tick tock, tick tock."

I hung up and head to my little flop near the Village, about one-third the price of my old place, getting by on my dwindling savings. Busting Mona presented itself as a double-edged sword. It could punch my ticket back uptown. Just as blowing it could park me on a street corner in the Bowery, or under a flat marker in a pauper's cemetery.

As I turned down the alley to the rear entrance, the rain swirled throwing a blinding wind in my face. I laughed, seeing myself as the moving eye of the storm, taking on the rough seas with the calm of an old fisherman, tall in his boat, riding out the waves by his lonesome.

Only suddenly, I wasn't alone.

Someone had crowded into my universe and even the heavy smell of wet cats and garbage couldn't hide the scent of a woman. She hovered in the mist, her face concealed under a wide brim black hat. I stopped and she glided forwarded a surreal vision, not walking, just floating. The hate and loathing ratcheted through my loins and I geared up to unleash it all, every ounce.

Then she was there, close, the hat tilted up, her full red lips pressed onto mine. The hate was over and I was back where I started.

She broke the kiss and the rain slackened. It was as if Nature too had had enough for one night and I said:

"Hello Mona."

The kiss had been nice while it lasted but it left a nasty taste in my mouth.

There were no words for what I felt. My shoulders hunched against the bitter cold sweeping my bones and I dove down into my soul for warmth but found nothing. So, I just stood waiting. Knowing that was exactly how she planned it. Exactly how she wanted to make contact, confident I'd fold like a flower at sunset. Jack Darwin went from climbing Redemption Mountain to sliding downhill into the muck in the space of one kiss.

"Can we talk?" she said simply. "Upstairs?"

I grunted something stupid and starting moving. We climbed the creaking stairs and went into my room. No keys in this joint; there was nothing worth taking unless you carried your booze in with you. Just the same I closed the door and threw the inside bolt. I switched on the lamp perched on my little kitchen table and the light filled the cracks in the plaster and bounced back at me with great reproach.

Mona doffed the ebon raincoat. Beneath it, she wore a plain black number showing more than it was hiding. She'd lost weight and her breasts looked smaller than I remembered but then how could anything measure up to what I remembered?

She curled onto the overstuffed couch. I straddled a kitchen chair with the dawning realization of what was happening. I buried my face in my hands and knuckled a thousand bright sparkles into my eyeballs. When I opened them Mona was still there, untangling her dark shoulder length locks with long painted fingers.

She smiled easily. "Not the best place you ever had."

"Not the best you ever kissed me."

"Touché, but since you didn't shoot me, I assume there's a chance you want to hear my side of things?"

"Damn it, Mona, cut the crap. You don't have a side."

"And damn it, Jack, I do."

I sat tall, subconsciously trying to dominate. My gut worked to recapture the hate I had nursed bottle to bottle, unwilling to believe it could dry up and blow away that fast. The hate had to be there lurking under the confusion wrought by her sudden and almost mystical reappearance. Maybe listening to Mona's *side of things* would bring it back. Sure, why not listen; I nodded and she started.

"I'm not going to lay a lot of grief on you about me being innocent or not betraying you. I won't even try. It happened, I did it and there's no going back or changing things. I am sorry, Jack, sorry what I did brought you to this." She let her head sweep the room. "I, I never thought it would be this hard on you."

I grimaced. "I should have been stronger, but then I thought I knew you."

"You did, Jack, as much as I'd allow any man to know me back then. What you didn't know was Tommy."

I frowned. The name scrambled from my ears to my brain and the frown grew into a deep growl. "You threw me in the ocean for another …

"For my son, Jack. For my son."

I don't know if a minute or a month passed as I sat there in stunned silence. At last, some words fell out of my mouth. "I don't understand."

"The first part is simple enough; I have a son. His father was a Marine who died in Iraq. From there it gets complicated. The boy and I lived with his grandfather. Lewis is my maiden name, Jack. I'm the widow of Gunnery Sergeant Leonard Brasno, Junior. Lenny Brasno is my father in law."

You think you're smart, that you have a leg up on the bad guys because they're dirty and you're clean. Only that's their real advantage. They don't run straight at you; they like to clip below the knees. It was a simple set up. Lenny Brasno had used his daughter-in-law like a loaded gun and his grandchild was the hammer.

I could feel the outline of the .45 in my pocket. It seemed to be catching fire, beckoning me. Mona's voice rose out of the background.

"It goes way back, Jack, before you and me. Detective Lima and the DA were closing in on Lenny's operations. When Levin mouthed off to me and I ran to you, Lenny got this big idea. He sent Jimmy Bones out with a proposal. I bait a trap that embarrasses the cops and the DA and blows up their case or, well …

"Your son dies?"

"Worse! Much worse, Jack." Mona shook head violently. "Lenny is the legal grandfather. He had natural rights to my boy and threatened to take him away. He promised to build up a phony case against me as an unfit mother. He had a dozen paid witnesses ready to prove it and …

"He had the lawyers and judges in his pocket to make it stick."

"What could I do?"

There was begging in Mona's voice that was irresistible. Just like before I felt compelled to listen, but I didn't have to believe. I could reserve that right for myself.

"That son of a bitch used my son to force me into prostitution. That's what it was, Jack. I was his whore and I did whatever it took to be with my son."

"Why pick on me and not Lima? He was the cop chasing him down. I didn't give a plugged nickel about Lenny Brasno until you walked through the door."

"He's thorough Jack. You don't survive and get to the top in the rackets doing things off-the-cuff. Lenny knew you and Lima were tight from the Gulf War. He had copies of your army profiles. You were the easy pick, the one he called … flexible."

A vile fluid ran down my throat, "I'll kill that bastard!"

"Will you, Jack? Will you kill him for me?"

Mona was on her feet moving towards

me, throwing her arms around my neck and fingering that throbbing scar in a way that made my face flush. I shook myself into focus.

"Let's slow it down. You got a nasty rep for double-crosses, baby. I need more. Let's start with a question. Say I buy you clearing town with your kid. Why take the disks? That had to be the piece set Brasno off, made him chase you. You could've dumped the jewels for money and kept on running, he might have let you go if he had the dirt back."

"I want my son back," Mona replied quietly. "I thought the disks might do it, you know what I mean. I guess I thought if I had them and Lenny didn't, I had leverage."

"Who killed Artie Levin?"

"Jimmy Bones."

"I still don't get what you want with me."

Mona sighed and drew a breath. "That's where it gets complicated. Jimmy Bones, Jack. He wants to make a run at Lenny; a big time run and Lenny knows nothing about it."

"What? How can you know that?"

Her eyes dipped, her lashes curled. "He told me."

"Told you?"

"Jimmy Bones was the one that found me, in New Orleans. He proposed a deal, the disks for my son but I had to work so his nose stayed clean. Brasno went down and Jimmy took over the organization nice and neat, no pushback from any of the soldiers."

"So now you're in bed with Jimmy Bones. You do sleep around."

Mona spun on me, all nasty and fired up. I took the slap and never blinked.

"I never slept with anyone but you Jack," she cried, stamping her foot. "I loved you, goddamn it." Her voice softened. "I still do."

There was a long pause, in which I sat silent. Too damn afraid of what I'd say to open my mouth. Then it just came out.

"But you loved your son more."

"What woman doesn't?"

I had no answer.

"So, you went to the German to try and buy in with a third party."

"I offered the jewels straight up for muscle."

Mona looked at me with those big, deep eyes and I had to turn away to keep a thousand and one old emotions from surging to the surface. She read it and came after me. She put her hands of my cheeks, turning my head to hers.

"You think I'm pretty don't you, Jack? Of course you do. Every man that's ever-laid eyes on me thinks it. I know it, so why lie about it. You get enough dirt thrown at you and you start to learn how to use what you have. Remember Froggy Lesner?"

"Sure, big guy, no neck, he's was one of Lenny's trigger men." I paused and added it up fast. My eyes got really narrow and my voice real low. "They found him in the Hudson with a belly full of slugs; a year ago wasn't it?"

Mona nodded and moved her mouth but I was way ahead of her. I'd run with these creeps a lot longer than her, so long it got where you started thinking like they did.

"Froggy was as sweet on you as every-one else." I said it bitterly. "Froggy had the brains of a tree slug and you used him to get your kid out of Lenny's house and lift the disks off Jimmy. Lenny figured it out and killed him. I'm betting old Froggy never had a clue what was on those disks."

"I told him it was about the custody hearings."

I was shaking my head.

"In his own perverted way, Jack, Brasno loves his grandson. I think he wants the kid back more than the jewels or even the disks."

"You haven't said it but I take it Jimmy Bones has your boy now. He found you and grabbed the kid before making his proposition but you managed to run."

"I thought Hoffman could pull it together."

"Dumb Mona, sorry, but you just aren't in league with any of these clowns. The German used Benny Kolpin to find him muscle alright, but once he got the kid my guess is, he would then turn it right around and blackmail you for the disks even as Jimmy was doing. It's a character flaw in bad guys. They won't deal for what they figure they can take. It might have worked only Benny rats Hoffman out and that was that. It's really ironic too that Lenny sent Jimmy Bones to make the kill."

Mona looked terribly pale. Her head was swimming from the depth of it all. I asked:

"How the hell did you find me?"

Mona smiled softly. "Rust darling, rust. Hoffman spotted you at that deli. He was a cagey bird and you forgot it. I went there and Gansky gave me your address. You still have tips coming to you."

***

"**W**here are the disks and the jewels now?"

Mona let a shallow laugh pass her lips and her eyes brightened. "I never had them!"

"What?"

"I gave them to Jerry Fertman."

"Fertman? My old landlord?"

She nodded. "He's had them all along only he has no idea what he's holding."

There it was; feminine guile in all its glory.

"Give me your cell phone."

Mona complied, smiling happily. I smiled back but still kept a few loose ends to myself, just in case. I got my party without naming names and made my pitch. After hanging up I told Mona, "We cool here for an hour. Why don't you try and get some rest?"

"I am exhausted," she admitted and so did manage to nod off.

I hung my suit in the shower to dry and sat around in my skivvies waiting, far too wired to nap. Or so I thought. When next her phone rang, I nearly hit my head on the ceiling. I snapped it up and almost immediately shut it down. Mona was awake and at my side.

"Son of a bitch had the wrong number."

It was another ten minutes before the phone rang again. I cupped it to my mouth and told Mona, "This is it." I listened a few moments more and then told her, "Hat and coat babe, we're on the move."

We went downstairs and out the back. A cool mist still covered the night as we made the street and hailed a cab.

"Jack, what the hell is going on? You're

acting very mysterious, like you don't trust me."

"Can you blame me?"

Mona suddenly looked terribly small and withered, not nearly as alive as she had in the alley those few short hours before. All the pent-up emotion, the fury and the despair, seemed to flow out of her body in a giant wave. All I could do was hope that despite my precautions and my better judgment she wasn't once more waltzing me out to the middle of a condemned bridge ready to cut the cables.

Harry met us outside the station. I had expected a phalanx of cops in riot gear. He was alone. Mona, realizing what I had done, that I'd called in the cavalry, cowed, blinked her eyes and held my hand. I won't pretend the reunion was cordial. Harry, noting the holding of hands, tossed me a circumspect stare as if to say: *Wasn't once around the maypole enough for you Jack?*

There wasn't time for a debate.

We went into his office and grabbed chairs, Harry at his desk and Mona pulling her folding chair up to my knees.

I asked, "You find it, Harry?"

He nodded. "There was a banana crate full of her crap stuffed in the super's base-ment. Yeah, we found it. It was all there like she said."

Mona pulled away staring at me. "How, how in the … you said nothing over the phone."

"Sorry, you slept and I sent a text."

From the look on Mona's face, I was certain she wished she could've flipped me to the gutter like a cigarette butt. But there were those loose ends to tighten. "I had to know if you were lying to me."

Mona was acquiescent. "So, we're square, is that it?"

"That's it. Now we get your son and finish off both Bones and Brasno."

Harry grinned. "Not we buddy, me. This is where you cut out. Mona makes her statement; the DA gets the marching order from a judge and we hit Brasno."

I scowled hard. "And what the hell am I supposed to do?"

"For starters go see Fertman. He said he was renting you that space in his closet as a personal favor. You owe him two bills."

I grinned. "Yeah, I'd like to see his face when I tell him there was a cool million in small gems in that pile."

"He says you got lucky Cinderella, the clock was striking midnight and the old buzzard planned to dump it with the next trash."

"Where's the stuff now?"

"The jewels are in evidence as are the disks. I viewed enough to know they're dynamite." He turned to Mona, his face suddenly softening. "Mona, if we'd known about the boy …

Mona sobbed, though Harry's words seemed to offer her a world of relief. Harry turned to me, reached out, and slapped a small black wallet into my palm. I didn't have to flip it open. I could feel the shield pressing the leather. Then he got very offi-cial, by the book.

"Mr. Darwin, your license is renewed for twenty-four hours. You will need to see a judge if you wish to permanently reinstate it. Ms. Lewis, I need your sworn statement on the authenticity of the jewels and the disks to get a warrant on Lenny Brasno's estate." She nodded. Harry looked squarely at me. "It gets done right, by the book. We follow the rules and the bad guys fall."

"And I land on my feet?"

"You get the chance, it's up to you."

"What about the kid?"

Harry shook his head. "That's the wrinkle you don't have. Jimmy Bones has already delivered the boy to his grandfather. We don't know his game but apparently he got advised by counsel to do it."

"Darius Edwards?"

"Yes. Like I said, we play this by the rules." Harry faced Mona who sat in shock, appalled at these unexpected developments. "You pulled the first run away when there were legal proceedings on the books against you. Brasno, as legal grandfather, still has a case against you as does the state over Artie Levin."

My back went up. "But …

"Easy, big guy, I said we do it legal. Once the courts finishes with Brasno and those disks, everything else will crumble. The DA said he'd take on Mona's case personally. He'll drop all charges and Mona can pursue full custody."

I looked at Mona. "Harry's right. Edwards and the rest of Brasno's lawyers can paint all the phony pictures they want about you but those disks will send him away for a long time and no jury in the world will believe that crap against you is anything but perjury."

Mona nodded, tears tipping her lashes. Harry took her by the arm to find a steno. I didn't follow them.

Mona cried worriedly. "Stay with me, Jack."

"Harry will hold your hand. I've got something I have to do."

"Like what?" Harry demanded fiercely. "What could you possibly have to do now?"

I looked at Mona. "Pay off my landlord and see if he's got a vacancy big enough for three. By the way Harry, can you spot me two hundred?"

***

I had my badge back and my edge.

To keep them I had to be more than just a PI again. I had to be a man without cops and judges propping me up under the armpits. There was one more mile to walk and I had to go it alone or not at all.

You see Harry read me the rules but knew damn well I'd always been a rule breaker.

It took me twenty minutes to taxi over to Lenny Brasno's big estate on Long Island on fifty of what Harry loaned me. To hell with Fertman, the notoriety he'd get in the press was payment enough for that extortionist. There was a phone at the gate but the iron was unlocked so I entered and proceeded up the gravel drive taking no notice at all of the colorful and expensive landscaping. Brasno had twenty-four-hour security so the welcome mat meant either I was expected or I was intruding. Maybe both for like the gate the ornate front door stood open, jammed that way by an over-sized dead body.

Another kind of rule breaker is a snitch. It was certain as a woman loves chocolate someone at headquarters was on Brasno's payroll. Maybe more than one and the word had swiftly gone out Mona was in custody. Harry knew it but his rules wouldn't allow him to voice his concern. What Brasno

Gun out, I advanced, the hardwood floors clicking under my heels. I crossed the long foyer to the mahogany staircase, iron rails bleeding off to the right.

knew, Jimmy Bones knew. My guess was the knives were out, literally, war was in the open now and it made me sweat.

Gun out, I advanced, the hardwood floors clicking under my heels. I crossed the long foyer to the mahogany staircase, iron rails bleeding off to the right. Trouble came out of a room to the left.

I didn't see the first guy but I intuitively sensed him, managing to halfway avoid the descending gun butt aimed at me head. It caught my scalp a glancing blow. It would have split my skull had it connected full force. Though buckled at the knees I spun on my heels and buried a fist in the guy's fleshy midsection. He bent and as I dropped my own .45 hard on his crown, I saw the second man drawing a bead on my brain. We fired simultaneously.

Under a small cloud of acrid smoke chocking my lungs, I stood unscathed, alone, the survivor. My heart raced, adrenaline pumping a new poise into my soul. I breathed through my nose and the sweat dried. My heart ticked steady as a Rolex. From here, I told myself, it was all about character. Who lived, who died.

A quick search of the hoods turned up two guns. The dead guy's .38 I emptied and sailed out the front door. The second man had small caliber .22 that I concealed

up my sleeve. Call it backup.

I took the gradually winding staircase two steps at time arriving at the midpoint of a long, carpeted hallway. With two doors to my left and three to my right my move was toward the last one on the right, the biggest door with the most elaborate frame; the one with the most *character*. I turned the brass handle and went in. Two bodies clogged my advance while lying face up on the enormous four-post bed was a third. Lenny Brasno stared at me through unseeing blank eyes, a single round hole in the center of his forehead. I'd been too late for that showdown but somewhere in the cavernous mansion, his killer waited my pleasure; and ten to one he held Tommy Brasno hostage.

I turned back into the hall and at the head of the stairs raised my voice.

"No good, Jimmy … you're boys are out of the loop. You'll have to face me one on one."

Almost immediately, the far-left door opened and a boy of about seven in rolled jeans and gray sweatshirt stepped into view. You could not miss his mother's dark hair and oversized eyes. Tommy Brasno looked glassy-eyed near to shock. Emerging behind him, gun protruding around the boy's ear, was Jimmy Bones.

I took a step forward.

"That's far enough," Jimmy hissed. "Let me see your hands." I raised them shoulder level as he ordered. "Throw your gun down the stairs."

I obliged and sent it bounding down to the lower floor.

"Why the gun, Jimmy. A knife has always been more your style?"

Jimmy grinned. "For certain occasions, yes, but Brasno and I had nothing to talk about. Not like Hoffman. It was slow going with him but I got everything I wanted."

"Like Mona's cell number."

He looked puzzled and I let it slide.

"So, you fed Lenny just enough lies for him to call and order me out here. Bring Mona and the jewels, he said." I grinned. "I told Mona it was a wrong number. Hell, poor Lenny probably hung up all giddy at the way things were turning around. He knew nothing about the disks. Hoffman did, so he you checked him out. All that left was getting the disks back. But once you knew the cops had them, you opted for hardball. My guess is beyond the dope on Lenny, they contained all kinds of contacts and information Brasno had on the payroll and you planned to use as blackmail; cops, judges, maybe higher. Am I right?"

"Good work Darwin," he wheezed, struggling for air in smoke blackened lungs. "Smart the way you figured that out."

"So, you killed Lenny and waited for me to show and take Mona the word. She shuts up or the kid gets hurt. It's not happening like that Bones. I'm leaving here with the boy and, if you're still alive, the cops will show and pick up the pieces."

He shook his head, letting his snake eyes roll around in his head gathering venom.

"No chance, Darwin. You see, with Brasno dead I need a fall guy. It's you the cops are going to find dead here, next to the Leech, with the gun that killed him in your hands."

"I've got half of City Hall on the way."

"And risk the kid? Bad bluff. I thought about that angle but counted on that wounded manhood of yours. I knew it wouldn't be enough just to clear your reputation; you had to get your mojo back, didn't you? OK, we'll do this the hard way. *Louie!"*

The first door behind me opened fast and bodies poured forth. I whirled on the lead gun, a guy with a bandaged nose and blackened eyes. Louie was the hood I'd worked over with the breadbasket. He was wearing a crooked grin and a look of anticipation. His type always smirked when they thought they had the upper hand. It went out the window with the shell I lodged in his throat from that .22 stuffed up my sleeve. He died wearing the most stupid, 'what in the hell just happened' expression you ever wanted to see.

I dropped and shot the second guy from right between Louie's legs, blowing out a kneecap. He was down and writhing, useless. I rose and got my own jollies watching my foot furrow a red streak across his mouth before getting caught on an ear.

In the dim part of the brain where the real world congregates, I heard the hammer of Jimmy's gun fall. I dropped but a slug ripped across my left shoulder, letting blood. I rolled behind an improvised shelter of Jimmy's fallen soldiers and the guy with busted knee took the second slug in his chest. That stopped his screaming.

Using the damn kid as a shield, Jimmy Bones backed into the room from whence he'd come. Ignoring the roaring hurt in my arm, I darted after him. The hidden gun had been a neat trick but now the rust was showing. Jimmy had already fully withdrawn and I thoughtlessly stood framed in the opening a painted bull's-eye facing a heartless killer. The intoxication in Jimmy's eyes shone like a revelation. The creep had me unless I shot through the kid.

But I couldn't and didn't have to because the kid saved me.

Maybe it was the inherited guts of a Marine that had Tommy Brasno kick back hard into Jimmy's shins. There couldn't have been much pain, but there was just enough surprise and outrage to create a moment of hesitation. A window just wide enough for me to leap through the doorway, landing a crushing rolled fist into Jimmy's teeth and gums. The gun dropped to the floor along with Jimmy Bones.

"Nice job, kid," I said grinning. Only Tommy Brasno was not finished being a hero.

"Look out!"

It was the goon I'd pasted downstairs. He must have had the head of a tank to be awake and back in the fray. He stormed into the room with my own damn gun extended. But he was in too close. I batted his arm down and the bullet buried in the floor. Then we closed, me slapping a fist over his gun hand. His protruding belly covered our hands like an oven mitt. Inside the folds, feeling the angles, I squeezed the trigger. The guy grunted and bled all over himself before titling left and going down.

Behind me, on the floor, Jimmy Bones was scrambling for his gun. I grabbed Tommy and hissed in his ear, "Get out of the house," then threw him bodily out of the room and slammed the door shut. Jimmy Bones and I were one on one.

Jimmy had his gun back but so what. He was a punk with little or no real backbone. I was ex-army wearing my balls on my sleeve. I should have told him bullets always fly straight. For when wild eyed and sweating Jimmy Bones fired, I just casually curled around them and, holding the dead punk's gun steady, hardly bothering to aim, blew Jimmy's weapon away along with three fingers.

Wheezing morbidly because he couldn't scream like a normal animal, Jimmy grabbed at his injured extremity and went to his knees where all he could do was bleed and whimper. I stepped in and put five fingers around his neck, jacking him back to his feet, digging in with a lust that had my whole body joining the party. It was venal and ugly and everything I needed to feel good about myself.

I laughed when he begged and let one hand go so I could smash him in the face. It broke his jaw and his mouth left a slimy coating of cartilage on my knuckles. Jimmy was crying now, begging and threatening all at once. I nearly pulled one ear off his head to keep his face straight and then casually put my gun in his mouth. His good hand pounded at me, clawing at my injured shoulder. I butted his head and the fingers fell away like cobwebs in a wind.

Jimmy was making little bubbling noises and the hate I had held so long, so hard, released, soaring free. I was alive and reveling in the slow death and devastation that I wrecked on the guy that had caused me so much pain. One more minute and …

"Jack! Stop, for the love of God! Stop!"

It was like a wail coming up through a fog. I barely heard it but I understood it and it cut the blood haze around my senses. Almost unconsciously, I dropped Jimmy Bones to the floor. He lay in a heap gurgling and crying as I turned to the now open door.

Mona stood there in doorway with her son pressed to her bosom, one hand awkwardly holding one of the guns from the bodies in the hall. They were both in tears, the kid with joy, and Mona, I didn't really know, perhaps a mix of emotions wildly drawn from the slaughter around her.

Downstairs, I heard bodies crashing through the house and coming up the stairs in the unmistakable scratch of heavy boots and leather riot gear.

Suddenly Mona's eyes flew wide. The gun in her hand flew up and fired. The heat whistled past my ear. I heard an ugly plop as it dug into soft flesh. I turned and watched Jimmy Bones' head tilt left with the weight of the heavy slug pushed through his heart and out his back, the ugly knife in his right hand clattering to the floor.

That was when Harry Lima burst onto the scene and all he could do was swear. I faced Mona who stood equally frozen, the gun still balanced stiffly in the air. I gently pushed her arm down and took her in my arms, her and the kid.

"It's OK, it over. It's all over."

***

It took almost four hours to finish answering Harry's questions, get the lab rats packed up and clear the house from cop to corpse to coroner. Even so, I had to swear to Harry I'd be downtown in the morning to make a statement.

"For most guys, this would cinch your loosing that badge, but I don't know. I think if you promise the D.A. to make him the Mayor next year, you'll come out alright."

"You knew I was coming here didn't you?"

"Like I told you already, you were the one went on a bender, not me."

Another hour went south while Mona put her son to bed in the now quiet and empty house. The doc had left some pills to help. Alone at last, Mona and I went down to the kitchen and made some coffee. She looked at me with a weak smile.

"I knew too, Jack."

"You did?"

"A wrong number that left you flushed under the collar? Then borrowing two hundred dollars to pay the rent? Nice dodge but haven't you learned anything through all this? A man never knows when the love of his life is lying. But a woman, she *always knows*. Detective Lima traced the number and you should have heard him cursing."

"My bad, I missed that trick. Guess I am rusty at that."

"Guess you are at that."

Suddenly, to my surprise, there was a knock on the kitchen door.

"Who the hell is that," I growled moving over slowly and opening it up.

(Continued on page 123)

ART: CLAYTON HINKLE

Welcoming Amethyst Eyes

BY STEVEN L. ROWE

When the woman stepped into sight, he should have been surprised, yet he was not. He knew there were men in that strange, unknown land. Where there were men, there were women, as naturally as night following day. Not women like that one though, he was certain of it. Women like that one were rare anywhere.

Seeing her put Ranulfr at ease. Seeing her *there,* of all places, though, was more than just putting him at ease. The sight of a woman such as she would have put any man at ease, truth be told.

Bold she was, unafraid, nor had *she* any reason to fear.

Clothed only in her own beauty, without a single garment or even ornament, yet armed with spear and shield she handled with the ease of one born to such trappings of battle. She stood at the edge of the clearing and watched Ranulfr, a slight smile at the corner of her perfect lips. Behind her, partially hidden by tall bushes, her horse chomped at the grass with a show of equine boredom. The horse, too, should have surprised Ranulfr, for he had not seen any sign of such creatures on this shore, so distant from his homeland. Yet the horse, to him, in the moment, was a natural as the woman.

Almost without thought, Ranulfr swung his shield arm out behind him, using the iron rim to smash in the teeth of the little warrior attacking from that direction. He did not need to look back to see the copper-skinned savage swept back by the blow, nor did he need to see if the man was dead. The sound of the attacker's neck snapping had been clear to Ranulfr's ears. One less skraeling to worry about.

The dark green of the forest behind her made her skin seem pale as milk. Her hair fell loose to her slender waist, save for a single long braid on either side that framed her face. A golden frame, as fitting for those perfect features as any could be.

Ranulfr would have been hard pressed to say what made her face so perfect. The high forehead under a sweep of gleaming golden hair? That straight nose, just a touch snubbed at the end? Perhaps those lips, cool, controlled, and yet inviting at the same time? Cheeks with a bare touch of color to hint at the emotion she was hiding?

No, if he had to choose, it would be her eyes. Even at the long distance, he could tell her eyes were remarkable, even for one such as her. Clear, deep amethyst like a shadowed mountain lake, and so large as to be almost inhuman.

A man could drown in those cool depths and never suffer a moment of regret. Jewels beyond price, those eyes. If a man had enough red blood in his veins to be called a man, he would dare any adventure to possess such a treasure.

The axe in his hand dripped with the blood of half a dozen of the ferocious red warriors. His mail had been rent by their jagged stone weapons, the leather beneath torn, and his flesh bruised. Nearly a score of the savages lay scattered about, twisted from the brutal wounds that had laid them out stark and cold, the work of Ranulfr and his comrades.

But those companions also awaited the coming of the ravens, each cut down, despite their valor, by the sheer number of their attackers. They had been six, not all that long ago. The attack had come without warning, arrows streaking out of the dark pine forest they trudged through. Most of the crude enemy shafts had been rebuffed by armor or blocked by shields. After the first encounter, three dozen painted savages had come screaming out of the woods and the bloody battle was joined.

Knut had gone down first, slowed by a flint-tipped arrow in his thigh so that a screaming savage could get close enough to use a polished wooden war club to shatter his skull. Still, the wily old reaver had gutted two of the attackers and neatly sliced an arm from a third before taking his death wound.

Svein had cut down Knut's copper-skinned killer while the attacker still shouted his triumph, only to have a stone-headed lance pierce his own worn hauberk from the side. Clutching his fatal wound, brave Svein had chopped the legs from another of the maddened attackers before finally being brought down under a flurry of blows from stone axes.

Wulf, Haakon and Olaf also had found their deaths that day. Better deaths than Randolf, Sigur and the others of their crew had found during the storm, at least. Better to die in battle than to be taken by the sea,

STEVEN L. ROWE is a former soldier who was stationed in West Germany during the last years before the end of the Cold War. His parents had followed the advice of Horace Greely and kept "going west", first from Pennsylvania to Ohio, and then to the foothills of Colorado. He spent many of his formative years exploring the old mining camps and ghost towns that dot the high country of Colorado. He is an amateur student of history, with interests ranging from Viking culture to the American west. After decades living in Colorado, he moved to central Florida to be closer to the ocean he has grown to love. Currently he is employed as an electronics technician in central Florida. He is the author of six novels and several short stories.

even on this strange shore, so far from the eyes of the Gods. Out of three score of good warriors, only six had survived the long storm and the wreck of their dragonship on the rocky coast of a land they had only heard of in fantastic tales.

They had been sailing south for a summer of raiding when the storm blew up. It was as if all the Gods had turned their back on them, all save Ran, the cold-hearted Goddess of the Sea, and she held only malice in her heart for those six reavers. Ranulfr had cause to wonder, as their ship pitched upon the black waves, what they had done to so offend her.

Without much of a plan, and even less hope, the six Vikings gathered what they could from the wreckage. Rather than follow the coast southward, they decided to strike out to the west. The storm had driven them in that direction. The wind and waves tried to force them onto the rocky shore in that direction. To them, it seemed obvious that the Norns had a fate awaiting them in the west, so to the west they went in search of their doom.

Five days they marched west, through a land rich in game. At no time did they see a single sign they were not alone in those dark forests and bountiful meadows. Not a footprint, not a voice, not a trace. Still, they knew hostile eyes watched them; for all that, they saw and heard nothing to indicate other men were about.

It came as almost a relief to be attacked by the skraelings. At least their foes were mortal. They might all die, but it would be in battle against men. Haakon and Olaf had started to speculate they were in a land of trolls or ghosts. Facing a horde of shrieking, bloodthirsty savages was far easier than walking in fear of the unknown.

The woman had appeared from among the pines after Olaf had gone down with his throat gaping open. The flint knives of the savages were of little value against the iron rings of their hauberks, but they cut naked flesh better than a razor. It was only when the last of his companions had tasted death that she had come forth for Ranulfr to see.

There was boldness in her casual stance. Her right foot planted firmly on the ground, her left leg forward, slightly bent, weight on the ball of her foot, she seemed ready to spring forward at any moment, yet she remained motionless save for the calm rise and fall of her breasts.

Ranulfr was no callow youth. He had known many women in his adventurous life. Far to the east, across the sea, he had left a wife with a swelling belly and three children to care for. During raids, he had availed himself of fiery Irish warrior-women, English farm-maids and even the weeping, praying Brides of the White Christ a time or two.

Yes, he knew women well, and in all his life, he had never seen one to equal *her*. That proud, beautiful head upon the white column of her neck, shoulders muscular and feminine, arms shapely and strong, hands with long, delicate fingers. A pair of breasts that were as full and firm as those of a girl just coming into womanhood above a slender waist and generous hips. Thighs trim and muscular, calves shapely and smooth, leading down to perfect ankles and strong, flawless feet.

She stood with her shield turned slightly to her rear, hiding no line of that magnificent form. She wanted Ranulfr to see her, to see *all* of her, in those few moments.

And see her he did, even while he fought on. The outcome of that day was already foretold. Ranulfr knew and accepted it without qualm. Moreover, he understood she knew the ending of the battle fully as well as he did.

Without his companions to distract the foe, the remaining skraelings came at him as a mob. At least he did not have to be concerned that he might tangle with one of his friends. Around him were none who did not wish his death.

Two of the savages gripped his shield, trying to drag him off balance. A third rushed from the front only to have his painted cheeks and nose laid open by a swept of his axe from left to right. Another pair of the savages had waited for just such a blow, pouncing on his arm and trying to wrestle the axe from his hand.

A sixth warrior charged past the shrieking, dying man Ranulfr had maimed, a stone-headed club poised to fall. That fellow looked to be a champion among the skraelings. Half a head taller than his fellows and correspondingly broader and heavier, his head was plucked bald save for a topknot of hair decorated with tall feathers. The old-copper color of his face had been painted with a broad black stripe across the eyes and vertical black stripes down both cheeks. Besides the lethal war club, he held a long flint knife in his left hand. The savage grinned in anticipation as he brought the club down with all his strength.

Ranulfr had faced such a situation before, though never without companions near at hand. For all their ferocity, none of the savages were large men. Only that champion of theirs stood higher than his shoulder. And it was clear they had no conception of the giant's strength a Viking like Ranulfr possessed.

He allowed the two tugging at his shield to pull him in their direction. At the same time, he threw his entire strength into pulling against the pair struggling for his axe. His muscles and tendons burned from the strain as he pulled both men from their feet and brought them up before him.

The stone club could not be stopped or slowed in its lethal fall. The face of the man wielding it changed from triumphant to horrified as his blow smashed into the skull of one of his own companions. The second men struggling for that axe lost his grip and stumbled past. Ranulfr hooked the edge of his weapon into the man's throat and ripped it open has he went by.

She seemed to lean forward slightly, wide amethyst eyes taking in every brutal motion. Was he wrong, or did the rise and fall of those coral-tipped breasts increase? She strove to appear calm and unmoved, yet to his eye, it seemed the battle awoke deep emotions within those perfect breasts.

Rather than struggle over the shield, Ranulfr simply released the grip and deftly slipped his arm from the straps. The pair of savages tumbled backward with their useless prize. The Viking stepped back a pace, drawing his sax with his left hand.

The skraeling champion pushed past the pair of dead men, one killed by his own hand, the other by Ranulfr. He was ready to claim a prize of his own, the death of the last of the white strangers. Ranulfr met him, blade for blade and axe to club.

At that, she did take a pace forward, a flush on her face, her lips parted to reveal perfect white pearls of teeth. Her smile grew slightly wider as the two men fought.

Ranulfr was the larger and the more powerful, a bear of a man, while the skraeling with faster, quick and vicious as a wolf. Like a wolf, he had others to distract the bear during the fight.

Even for Ranulfr, Viking that he was, that battle was epic. Early on, the blade of his iron axe met full against the stone-headed club of his principle foe. Hard stone split and the pieces slipped from the sinew wrapping that held them. At the same time, the iron blade shattered, leaving Ranulfr with a jagged-edged club rather than the keen weapon that he was an expert with.

At that exchange, she moved yet another pace nearer to the combat, the lean muscles of her stomach tight with excitement, her breath coming swiftly, her checks crimson and her eyes bright. Emotion surged through her body, making Ranulfr lust for her even more. Soon, soon, the fight would reach the inevitable ending, and he would receive the reward her presence promised.

Stone hatchets in copper hands smashed at his hauberk, parting rings, tearing at the leather, wool and flesh beneath. In reply, the razor edge of his sax cut deep into skin, muscle and bone. One of the red wolves was down, clutching at his entrails. Another howled in darkness, both eyes raked away by a blow from the jagged iron stump of Ranulfr's axe. The blood that washed in a torrent down his ruined face promised that he would not howl for long.

The red wolves howled, ripped at the white bear and died under his response to their teeth and claws. For all the damage they did, the bear still stood and fought. In time, all that the red wolves could remember was their battle. Nothing else mattered to those who still drew breath. For the bear, *she* still remained foremost in his thoughts.

For Ranulfr, there were three constants left in the world: The gloomy darkness of the pine forest where he fought, the white-toothed grimace of the skraeling warrior before him and the gleaming white and gold promise of *her*. His mail hung in tatters from his giant frame. The leather beneath, and the wool beneath that were likewise torn and bloody, much of the blood pumping from Ranulfr himself.

Of the red wolves, only one remained. All the others had fallen beneath the keen blade or iron club that Ranulfr wielded with superb skill. Quick and lithe, that foe still bore a dozen cuts and scrapes, though none dangerous. Ranulfr could not say the same. The blood poured from his right shoulder, making it hard to keep his grip on the broken axe. The blade of a flint knife was jammed in one of his ribs and when he coughed, a bloody froth came to his lips. Other wounds were hidden under the wreckage of his armor and breeches, some deep enough to promise death if they were not staunched soon.

The painted warrior sneered, certain of victory. In all truth, Ranulfr was surprised such a victory had not already come. Still, an ending could not be far off. Exhaustion set Ranulfr's muscles to trembling. Loss of blood made it difficult to stand or to see clearly. To be certain, he had little strength left to him. The bloody shambles all around the two combatants was far better than the Viking had expected, he thought to himself with a degree of satisfaction.

It was obvious *she* was surprised as well, and somewhat disquieted. Spear and shield had been dropped as she moved closer. She kneaded her strong hands together in her agitation. Stern resolve kept emotion from her features. Ranulfr noted her cheeks had gone pale and understood what it was she feared.

The savage came in quick and hard, striking with a stone axe in each hand, weapons he had snatched from the bloody field to replace those already broken in the battle. Ranulfr countered each blow as best he could, guiding the chipped stone edges past his body to right and left by bare inches. Back and back and back he was forced as the savage goaded himself into greater and greater fury.

A thrust from the notched sax was met by a blow that sent the blade spinning from Ranulfr's hand. A desperate slash from the ruined axe was hooked aside by one hatchet, followed by a blow from the other that gashed his arm to the bone and lost him the weapon.

Ranulfr retreated wearily, stumbling as the woman looked on, suddenly alert. The skraeling stalked after him, the red wolf closing in, ready to tear out the throat of the dying bear. Three paces backward,

four, five. And then Ranulfr's foot struck against the corpse of one of his companions and he went down, arms flung wide.

That was the moment the savage champion had been waiting for. With a laughing snarl, he hurled himself on his prone enemy, aiming his hatchet to part the sweaty blonde mat of hair revealed when Ranulfr's helmet fell away from his head.

It was the moment Ranulfr had been waiting for as well. The end of the battle, the finish foredoomed. As he hoped, as he planned, the fingers of his left hand brushed the blade that Knut had dropped in death. Fingers touched the blade near the hilt, hand grasped that hilt and with the last of his strength, Ranulfr swung that blade up and around, allowing the skraeling to be his own executioner and impale himself on the bloody steel, his own final blow unstruck.

It took many long minutes for Ranulfr to roll that body of his last foe from where it had fallen across his chest. More long minutes for Ranulfr to rise to his feet, turn and see that she still stood there, shocked by the finale of the fray.

Wonder and dismay fought to shatter her calm expression. Those magnificent breasts were still as she forgot to breathe. Those eyes, those incredible amethyst eyes, were wide in admiration for his fighting ability, wide in fear for what his victory meant.

There were words Ranulfr wished that he could speak. Words to comfort her, to apologize for his victory and the fear it caused her. An attempt to draw breath for those words induced a fit of coughing,

(Continued on page 122)

A Tale of Two Stories
BY DAVID GOUDSWARD

*The complicated publishing histories of
C.L. Moore's "Werewoman" and Henry S. Whitehead's "The Tree-Man"*

In August 1989, Tor released the Karl Edward Wagner edited anthology *Echoes of Valor II*. The hardcover reprints nine classic pulp SF/F short stories with notes on each story's background. One of the stories was a C. L. Moore Northwest Smith tale, "Werewoman." The acknowledgments cite a 1938 copyright by Moore for the story,

with a 1966 renewal. Neither copyright claim is valid. The Moore estate insisted on the wording, the final salvo in her feud with Sam Moskowitz that had been raging for decades. In fact, the introductory notes to the stories were written by the petulant Moskowitz. Moore, had she not died in 1987, would probably have rescinded permission to print the story before allowing Moskowitz to be involved.

Moore had given the story to Robert Barlow for his amateur publication *Leaves*. It appeared in the winter of 1938, the second (and last) issue. *Leaves II* was 64 mimeographed sheets, side-stapled with a tape-bound spine. Sixty copies were printed by Claire Beck at his Futile Press in Lakeport, California. Contributors reflect Barlow's integration into Lovecraft's circle. The table of contents is a veritable who's who of Lovecraft's correspondents. In addition to Moore, the issue includes Donald Wandrei, Vrest Orton, Frank Belknap Long, and Fritz Leiber, as well as posthumous selections from Lovecraft and Whitehead.

The story, among the earliest Northwest Smith story written, is distinctly different from the subsequent adventures of the hero. Smith is wounded in a battle on an unnamed planet and flees the expected looters by going into the badlands. There, he finds himself surrounded by a pack of female werewolves. The alpha she-wolf senses a kindred blood-thirsty spirit and saves him from her pack. Smith and the pack encounter a valley where a lost civilization is cursed to exist as ghosts. Smith destroys a grave marker, which is the source of a mist that traps the ghosts. After doing so, he awakens among a group of men, one of whom seems to recognize Smith's eyes as being similar to those of a wolf from the pack.

Moore may or may not have received a contributor's copy of *Leaves II*. If she did, she soon forgot about the story. More interesting is that Barlow, four years before *Leaves II,* had typed up three copies of

"Werewoman." He then bound at least one in half morocco with heavy paper-covered boards that he sent back to Moore.

So, when she and Kuttner could not find her typescript of "Werewoman," it may simply have been they were looking for loose papers, not a shelved book. Kuttner wrote August Derleth on May 1, 1948, thanking him for sending the typescript from Barlow. "She'd forgotten its existence, and I doubt if she'll ever reread it. Somehow one's old stories always look so God-awful — at least mine do, and Kat says hers do too." There is no way to determine if this is yet another typescript or one of the three Barlow had not bound.

Eight years later, in 1956, Kuttner, wrote to Moskowitz looking for information on "Werewoman," a story Moore still barely remembered. It appears that somehow, Kuttner and Moore had already lost the copy sent by Derleth.

Moore didn't remember it was her friend Barlow. All she remembered was giving it to an amateur journal but wasn't even sure if it was a fragment, a draft, or a completed story. Moore had just released a collection of Northwest Smith stories through Gnome Press and may have found notes on the forgotten tale.

Moskowitz provided Kuttner with Clyde Beck's address, the brother of Claire, who had printed *Leaves II*. They presented Moore with their only file copy. It was only then that Moore discovered Barlow had posted a copyright. Copyright law in 1938 required the copyright to be registered. Barlow never recorded the copyright. Moore had already released two collections of her work through Gnome Press. Since there was no new collection in the works, there was no pressing need to verify the registration. Moore decided it was easier to just wait until 1966 when the copyright would expire and then renew the story under her own name.

Moskowitz was working for *Fantastic,* looking for reprint (i.e., inexpensive) stories. An unknown Northwest Smith story would be a coup for the magazine, so he atypically offered her a generous 2¢ a word for a one-time use. She refused, saying she had also misplaced the copy of *Leaves II* given her by the Becks. In 1963, he had moved on to *Amazing Stories* and asked again, having obtained his own copy to transcribe. She refused again, possibly believing the copyright was valid. Or she may not have liked the profiles he had written on her and her late husband in the magazine (Kuttner had died in 1958). This latter theory seems to have some validity. Soon after, she also refused to intervene when her agent and Moskowitz sparred off over the rights to Kuttner's "Twonky" for his latest anthology of robot stories.

Moskowitz had also noted the copyright, legitimate or not, ended in 1966. Without asking permission or offering payment, he published "Werewoman" in his *Horrors Unknown* anthology. He touted this 1971 collection as stories that he, as a "historian in the field of fantastic literature," had filled with forgotten stories of merit that he had located. By no coincidence, ten of the 11 stories were also out of copyright. Moskowitz believed in reprinting material out of copyright as it was the "right of any citizen to do so." The lack of any need to pay the authors was undoubtedly a factor as well.

"Werewoman" subsequently appeared in the 1973 anthology *The Edge of Never.*" The source listing in the front of the book reads "'Werewoman,' by C. L. Moore, originally appeared in Leaves, #2." Reprinted by permission of the author and her agents, Harold Matson Company, Inc." It circumvents the entire copyright issue and reinforces Moskowitz's use as unauthorized.

In addition to using "Werewoman" without permission, Moskowitz recycled the *Amazing Stories* profiles on Moore and Kuttner in *Seekers of Tomorrow,* a collection of his biographies from the magazine. Moore was not happy with Moskowitz and said so in no uncertain words when interviewed in 1976 for *Chacal,* a new and short-lived semi-pro fanzine:

I very foolishly ... gave it to a fan magazine who wanted to print it.... The error that I made there was I didn't realize they had copyrighted it. So twenty years later, who but Sam Moskowitz.... [ellipses original] uh, performed his usual, um, **practice** *[emphasis hers] of jumping on things two seconds after the copyright had lapsed! So he reprinted it, of course, without paying me anything for it. Incidentally, it is simply not a thing any other publisher I know of has ever done. I have had stories of mine printed after the copyright had lapsed and I've always been paid for them. Publishers just don't do things that way, but Moskowitz is an exception to the rule and nothing can be done about that!*

Moskowitz waited until 1979 to reply in *Fantasy Commentator 4,* no. 2. By amazing "coincidence," this was the

C.L. Moore

time when rumors began floating within the profession that Moore's historically poor memory was failing quickly. Fandom would not learn she had been diagnosed with Alzheimer's disease for several years. Moskowitz defended himself against Moore in the *Chacal* interview by attacking her faulty memory. He nitpicked her recollection of details and events that, even he had to admit, had taken place nearly 50 years earlier. And then reiterated the story was out of copyright and split hairs about copyright law as though he had a legal background. (His profession was editor of a frozen foods newsletter). His final argument was essentially an extended and more indignant version of the introductory notes he used *Horrors Unknown*. This was a retelling of how he found Kuttner and

Moore a source to obtain a *Leaves*. His "professional avocation" (his oxymoron, not mine) was researching obscure science fiction stories, and he had provided his vast expertise without remuneration. Supplying information so specific that Moore obtained the rare collectible for free, should count as a level of in-kind service that was more than adequate compensation to use the story. By the end of the rebuttal, his wounded ego is tangible.

By the time Karl Edward Wagner was compiling *Echoes of Valor II,* Moore had succumbed to Alzheimer's. Wagner dedicated the volume to her, and of the four authors featured, Robert E. Howard, Leigh Brackett, and Manly Wade Wellman, Moore is the most prominent. Moskowitz is asked to introduce two Moore stories, "Song in a

Minor Key" and "Werewoman."

"Song in a Minor Key" was another uncollected item that first ran in the fanzine *Scienti-Snaps* in 1940. His introduction to "Song in a Minor Key" is an unremarkable, bland collection of notes. But Moskowitz simply could not let go of the "Werewoman" challenge to his authority. His afterword is a brief reiteration of his version of events from *Fantasy Commentator*. He mentions her disease as the cause of conflicting dates and accounts, but still managing to keep the focus on his aggrievements.

Forrest Ackerman, who had also been involved in a public disagreement with Moore, did the afterword to Moore's "Nymph of Darkness" in the same book. He subtly and briefly addresses their spat over credit. He then shrugs it off, admitting with her mental deterioration, the point was now moot. His light-heartedness and casual deference make Moskowitz look all the pettier.

Moskowitz takes a shot at Barlow and *Leaves II,* falling back on the *Fantasy Commentator* stance that Moore should be grateful he used the story. After all, he congratulates himself, his use of "Werewoman" was its first professional publication. He doesn't elaborate on how not paying Moore for the unauthorized use of her story constitutes "professional."

Emphasizing *Leaves* was an amateur journal, he points out that "[u]nlike the first, all the material in the second issue — except a story by Henry S. Whitehead "The Tree-Man" — was original and that story heavily revised for the LEAVES printing." It appears to be a shot aimed at Barlow because only an amateur would revise a previously published text by a leading pulp figure like Henry S. Whitehead. But for all Moskowitz's self-proclaimed expertise, he was wrong about Barlow being the revisionist of "The Tree-Man." And "Werewoman" may have had complications far beyond those created by Moskowitz's self-absorbed arrogance.

In 1934, Moore sent Barlow the original "Werewoman" typescript. Farnsworth Wright, the editor of *Weird Tales,* had received so much positive feedback for her first story, "Shambleau," that Wright wrote to Moore requesting more Northwest Smith stories. Among them, she submitted "The Werewoman." Wright returned it asking for revisions. She wasn't surprised. In a letter to Barlow dated July 1, 1934, she admits it was "rather terrible." Wright had asked about revisions several times, but Moore was at a loss at how to rewrite it. By 1935, she had already sold several more stories to Wright ("Black Thirst" and "Scarlet Dream"), and revising it was not a high priority.

Barlow and Moore had been regular correspondents since his first fan letter in March of 1934. Their correspondence quickly became friendlier. They began loaning books to each other, and he began to consider compiling a collection of her stories from the manuscripts and typescripts she gifted him. Then he learned amateur publisher William Crawford had approached Moore to publish a collection of her stories.

Since Barlow had plans to release his own book of her stories, he recruited Lovecraft to contact Moore and try to dissuade her. Lovecraft had dealt with Crawford and was not impressed (Crawford would later publish "The Shadow over Innsmouth" as a book so ineptly that even the errata sheet had mistakes). Moore had her eye on the potential revenue, but Crawford's project quietly died. So did Barlow's, per usual, but he had the scripts.

"Werewoman" may have been one of the first he acquired from Moore. Barlow had asked for the manuscript of "Shambeau" soon after its publication, for his collection. She no longer had it and promised him others. It could have gone to Barlow as early as 1934 when Wright sent it back for revisions, but he doesn't mention it by name until 1935.

Later that same year, she also sends the carbons of "Werewoman" to Barlow and his houseguest, Lovecraft. She apologizes for sending the carbons, but she couldn't find the original typescript (which she had already sent to Barlow). By the time the carbons arrived, Lovecraft had departed the Barlow house in DeLand, Florida and returned to his beloved St. Augustine, timing his departure with the Barlow vacation in Daytona.

On August 24, Barlow left Daytona to tour St. Augustine with Lovecraft, bringing the carbons with him. They read the story in the covered market place in Plaza de la Constitución. Lovecraft agreed with Barlow's assessment — regardless of Wright's opinion, "Werewoman" was one of her best, right up at the top of her work with "Shambeau."

In September, Moore wrote a note to Barlow. She had finally come up with an idea to revise "Werewoman" for *Weird Tales* and requested he return the text so she could work on it. Apparently, she made the revisions and sent it to Barlow for his opinion. Barlow sent it to Lovecraft, who acknowledged its arrival in Providence on January 2, 1936. Lovecraft's comment carefully avoided mentioning the new version. Instead, he recalled reading the original in St. Augustine and, in a carefully phrased observation, said Barlow "got the good text," presumably for *Dragon-Fly 2*. However, Barlow would hold the publication another 2 years for *Leaves II.*

Any attempts to resubmit the story were forgotten in February when Moore's fiancé, Herbert Lewis, was accidentally killed while cleaning his gun, the standard euphemism for a suicide. A year later, Lovecraft died. The Moore-Barlow correspondence takes on a more sober note. However, her April 17 letter to Barlow also notes that Wright still wanted revisions that she hadn't made. With Henry S. Whitehead, Robert E. Howard, and H. P. Lovecraft dead, popular and reliable writers were scarce. Wright went so far as to ask Otis Kline to convince Moore to expedite the story. Kline, a literary agent, author, and collaborator with E. Hoffmann Price (another correspondent of Moore), had no better luck. She also declared Barlow is "still welcome to use the original," again suggesting there was a revised copy extant.

A June letter from Moore asked how *Leaves* was coming along and muses that she wished Virgil Finlay would do a drawing for "Werewoman." When *Leaves I* was released, Moore's story was not in it. Perhaps Barlow had pulled while writing to Findlay to see if he would contribute such a drawing. When "Werewoman" did appear in *Leaves II*, there were no illustrations — mimeograph is not the optimal medium for line art, as evidenced by the cover.

There is no record of the revised "Werewoman" in correspondence or publications per se. Perhaps Moore never bothered to make the final revisions Wright wanted. Her romance with Henry Kuttner was becoming serious. Her last story for *Weird Tales* appeared in the December 1939 issue as she focused on better-paying markets. Moore and Kuttner were married in 1940, the same year Farnsworth Wright was unceremoniously fired from *Weird Tales*. Even if Moore had sent the twice-revised story to *Weird Tales,* the new editor Dorothy McIlwraith was not likely to accept it. Northwest Smith was passé and hadn't appeared in the magazine for several years. A refusal after that much time and effort would be the end of "Werewoman" as far as Moore was concerned. The story would be discarded or filed away, forgotten until Kuttner wrote Derleth looking for a copy.

John McLaughlin offered Barlow's bound typescript "Werewoman" text in his 1984 *Book Sail* catalog. The actual history of the item is a mystery. He also notes a "few corrections to the text in a non-authorial hand, possibly Barlow's." Alternately, Barlow may have bound Moore's original typescript, the one returned by Wright, in which case the corrections could have been made inhouse in 1934 at *Weird Tales*. McLaughlin acquired it from noted collector Gerry de la Ree. It is inscribed to de la Ree by Moore. Whether de la Ree purchased the book and brought it to Moore to be signed, or Moore finally found the Barlow bound copy and regifted it to de la Ree is just the latest twist in a long saga.

The other story in *Leaves II* that Moskowitz dismissed was Henry S. Whitehead's piece, "The Tree-Man." It was indeed heavily revised, but if Moskowitz is inferring Barlow had done the revisions, Moskowitz was wrong.

Gerald Canevin recounts his first visit to St. Croix in "The Tree-Man," Whitehead's sixth story with his semi-biographic protagonist. Canevin would appear in an additional eight tales, including collaborations with HP Lovecraft and three posthumously published stories.

Canevin is amazed that he is considered a minor celebrity by virtue of being the great-nephew of a Scottish planter on the island in the 1870s. He goes to visit Great Fountain, the abandoned family estate. There he first encounters Silvio Fabricius, the man who spends his days listening to his tree. He learns that the villagers around Great Fountain are of pure Dahomeyan stock, originally refugees from the Haitian Revolution against French slaveholders in the 1790s. Left alone after Great Fountain was abandoned, the village had returned to their traditional Vodou. Fabricius spends his days embracing a great coconut palm tree and listening to the spirit, leaving his post only to relay messages to the village. (Whitehead's understanding of Dahomeyan Vodou is superficial but not entirely incorrect. Dahomey practiced a unique form that was a hybrid of animist traditions and Vodou practices).

When Great Fountain becomes a pineapple plantation, a simmering hatred of the tree-man by the plantation foreman begins

Henry S. Whitehead

to grow. Canevin witnesses these events, fearing the inevitable outcome. When it comes to pass, Gerard Canevin understands his beloved island is home to beliefs and powers that must be respected by the white population.

The story first ran in *Weird Tales,* February-March 1931. Whitehead, seeing it print, was dissatisfied with the final version. In October of that year, E. Hoffmann Price approached Whitehead about a project. He and Kirk Mashburn had decided to compile an anthology of weird fiction and then market it to a publisher. They had already agreed on stories by H. P. Lovecraft and Robert E. Howard. Now they were looking at Whitehead's "The Lips," originally published in *Weird Tales*, September 1929. Whitehead was amenable but thought he had several more recent pieces that might be more appropriate. By the time Lovecraft mentioned the anthology to Elizabeth Toldridge, at the end of 1932, the table of contents had changed. Price couldn't decide on which Lovecraft story to include, and Mashburn thought Whitehead was too longwinded to include. By 1933, Whitehead was dead, and his contribution had been removed. Even Robert E. Howard's story had been swapped out for another. The anthology never went beyond the planning stage.

While Price and Mashburn had been vacillating over the contents, Whitehead had begun editing "The Tree-Man," the latest choice for the anthology. The revisions were extensive, with Whitehead slashing entire passages.

The result was a story with tighter prose and a stronger opening. When Whitehead died November 23, 1932, E. Hoffmann

Price had the carbons.

Soon after Whitehead's death, Robert Barlow decided to solicit letters written by Whitehead for a small booklet as a memorial. Tentatively called *Caneviniana*, the project sputtered to a stop the next year. Most of the letters from such peers as Lovecraft, Clark Ashton Smith, and Robert E. Howard were eventually lost. In 1942, Barlow would provide Paul Freehafer the surviving 8 pages, already cut into mimeograph stencils. Freehafer then published those as *The Letters of Henry S. Whitehead* as a one-shot publication for the Fantasy Amateur Press Association. This booklet includes three letters Whitehead wrote to E. Hoffman Price in 1926.

Unaware *Caneviniana* was already faltering, Price sent more Whitehead material. A March 1933 entry in Barlow's diary notes he had just gotten Price to loan him "Henry S. Whitehead's Tree-Man in revised carbon and [a] letter written 2 weeks before his death." If the carbons and this letter were ever returned to Price or lost with the other material for the ill-fated booklet is irrelevant — they are now lost. But Barlow kept a copy of the Tree-Man revision, be it the original carbons or his own transcript.

The story ran in *Leaves II,* along with a checklist of Whitehead's published stories. Unlike "Werewoman" which has subsequently been reprinted without alterations, "Tree-Man" various appearances almost merits a variorum. The 1931 *Weird Tales* version was reprinted in a 1953 issue, and even that has revisions: British spellings were swapped out for the American, but not consistently. And Whitehead's use of Vodu was changed to Voodu. This is the only time the original version was reprinted.

Whitehead's revisions in the *Leaves II* edition were significant. On the first page alone, 200 words of 550 were excised. This is the edition that August Derleth used in 1944 for *Jumbee and Other Uncanny Tales*, the first Arkham House collection of Whitehead's stories, and, therefore, the de facto official version. This is not to say reprint the story was as simple as Barlow handing him the typescript. A quick glance at the copyright page of Jumbee subtly demonstrates the problem Derleth ran into. Derleth acquired the 14 stories as copyrighted by their original publishers — *Weird Tales, Adventure,* and *Strange Tales,* even though he didn't want the published versions with edits. He wanted the original typescripts. Barlow provided "The Tree-Man," but Whitehead's neighbor and a longtime friend had been given some of the manuscripts as mementos. The rest belonged to the estate, which went to Whitehead's father. When Whitehead's father died on February 28, 1937, he left his estate to his assistant. In addition to Henry H. Whitehead's estate, she thereby became the owner of Henry S. Whitehead's estate, including his literary estate. Derleth ended up having to give a percentage of the sales to the estate. *West India Lights,* the second Whitehead collection, would prove even more complicated.

All subsequent reprints of "The Tree-Man" are derived from the revision first published in *Leaves II* and reprinted by Arkham House in *Jumbee*. "The Tree-Man" would continue to appear in Whitehead

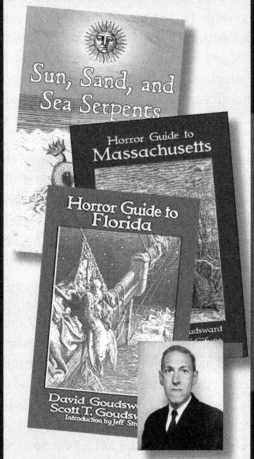
collections, mostly incomplete reprints of *Jumbee* and *West India Lights*, with minor tweaks. In fact, the only reprint of "The Tree-Man" with a significant change from the *Jumbee* is the 2020 *The Dragon-Fly and Leaves* book self-published by S. T. Joshi. There is a typo on Joshi's edition — "culius" when it should be "cultus" and a single odd word in a larger font in the middle of a sentence.

So, two tales by legendary *Weird Tales* authors barely survived to be appreciated today. Fortunately, their legacies were saved by their appearance in the amateur press of Robert Barlow, somewhat of a legend himself. Each story has a journey to literary immortality that is almost a weird tale unto itself. ∎

David Goudsward is the author of sixteen books, including *Sun, Sand, and Sea Serpents*, *The Westford Knight and Henry Sinclair*, and *H. P. Lovecraft in the Merrimack Valley*.

A retired librarian turned independent scholar, he has appeared on such television programs as *Secrets and Mysteries*, *Mysteries at the Museum*, and *Monumental Mysteries*.

He lives in southern Florida, where he is currently researching H. P. Lovecraft's visits to Florida and their influence on his works.

A Tale of Two Stories

Sources and further reading

Special thanks to Martin Andersson, Bobby Derie, Ken Faig, and Marcos Legaria

Ackerman, Forrest J. "Genesis of an Invisible Venusienne." In *Echoes of Valor II.* ed. Karl Edward Wagner. NY: Tor Books, 1989.

Barlow, Robert H. [1933 daily diary]. Kenneth W. Faig, Jr. archive on Robert H. Barlow, Ms.2018.019, Brown University Library.

The Book Sail 16th Anniversary Catalogue: Literature, Art and Artifacts That Will Forever Remain Among the Undead. ed. John McLaughlin. Orange, CA: McLaughlin Press, 1984.

Derie, Bobby. "A Lost Weird Anthology." In *Weird Talers: Essays on Robert E. Howard and Others.* New York: Hippocampus Press, 2019.

Kuttner, Henry. Letter to August Derleth. August William Derleth Papers, Wisconsin Historical Society.

Lord, Glenn. "The Price-Mashburn Anthology." *Zarfhaana* 7, August 1976.

Lovecraft, H. P. *Letters to C. L. Moore and Others.* ed. David E. Schultz and S. T. Joshi. New York: Hippocampus Press, 2017.

Lovecraft, H. P. *Letters to Elizabeth Toldridge and Anne Tillery Renshaw.* ed. David E. Schultz and S. T. Joshi. New York: Hippocampus Press, 2014.

Lovecraft, H. P. *O Fortunate Floridian: H. P. Lovecraft's Letters to R. H. Barlow.* ed. S. T. Joshi and David E. Schultz. Tampa, FL: University of Tampa Press, 2007.

Moore, C. L. "Interview: C. L. Moore Talks to Chacal." int. Byron Roark. *Chacal* 1, no. 1 (Winter 1976).

Moore, C. L. Letters to R. H. Barlow. H.P. Lovecraft Collection, John Hay Library, Brown University.

Moore, C. L. "Werewoman." In *The Dragon-Fly and Leaves.* ed. S.T. Joshi. Seattle: Sarnath Press, 2020.

Moore, C. L. "Werewoman." In *Echoes of Valor II.* ed. Karl Edward Wagner. NY: Tor Books, 1989.

Moore, C. L. "Werewoman." In *The Edge of Never - Classic and Contemporary Tales of the Supernatural.* ed. Robert Hoskins. Greenwich, CT: Fawcett Publications, 1973.

Moore, C. L. "Werewoman." In *Horrors Unknown.* ed. Sam Moskowitz. NY: Walker & Co., 1971.

Moore, C. L. "Werewoman." *Leaves II,* ed. R. H. Barlow. (Winter 1938).

Moskowitz, Sam. "C. L. Moore: Catherine the Great." *Amazing Stories.* August 1962.

Moskowitz, Sam. "The Immortal Storm, part 9." *Fantasy Commentator* 2, no .4 (Fall 1947).

Moskowitz, Sam. "The Immortal Storm, part 14." *Fantasy Commentator* 3, no. 1 (Winter 1948-49).

Moskowitz, Sam. "The Secret Lives of Henry Kuttner." *Amazing Stories*, October 1962.

Moskowitz, Sam. *Seekers of Tomorrow.* Cleveland: World Publishing Company, 1966.

Moskowitz, Sam. "Some Thoughts on C. L. Moore" *Fantasy Commentator* 4, no. 2 (Winter 1979-80).

Whitehead, Henry, S. The Letters of Henry S. Whitehead. ed. R. H. Barlow and Paul Freehafer. [Los Angeles]: The Fantasy Amateur Press Association mailing #22 (December 1942).

Whitehead, Henry S. "The Tree-Man." In *The Dragon-Fly and Leaves.* ed. S.T. Joshi. Seattle: Sarnath Press, 2020.

Whitehead, Henry S. *Jumbee and Other Uncanny Tale.* Sauk City, WI: Arkham House, 1944.

Whitehead, Henry S. "The Tree-Man." *Leaves II,* ed. R. H. Barlow. (Winter 1938).

Whitehead, Henry S. "The Tree-Man." *Weird Tales,* February-March 1931.

Whitehead, Henry S. "The Tree-Man." *Weird Tales,* September 1953.

Whitehead, Henry S. *West India Lights.* Sauk City, WI: Arkham House, 1946.

*The green-glowing eyes met his… and her keen,
moon-white face broke into a smile of hellish joy.*

ART: CLAYTON HINKLE

WEREWOMAN

BY C. L. MOORE

"Werewoman" first appeared in Leaves II, *the "amateur" publication from Robert Barlow, noted weird tale fan and friend of H.P. Lovecraft.* Weird Tales *turned the story down at least once, in spite of the overwhelming popularity of Moore's Northwest Smith stories. It is admittedly different from the other stories in the Smith collection, but the story's rediscovery was almost overshadowed by the subsequent feud between Moore and Sam Moskowitz. (See 'A Tale of Two Stories' by Dave Goudsward in this issue).*

With the noise of battle fading behind him down the wind, Northwest Smith staggered into the west and the twilight, stumbling as he went. Blood spattered brightly behind him on the rocks, leaving a clear trail to track him by, but he knew he would not be followed far. He was headed into the salt wastelands to the westward, and they would not follow him there.

He urged his reluctant feet faster, for he knew that he must be out of sight in the grey waste before the first of the scavengers came to loot the dead. They would follow—that trail of blood and staggering footsteps would draw them like wolves on his track, hot in the hope of further spoils—but they would not come far. He grinned a little wryly at the thought, for he was going into no safety here, though he left certain death behind. He was stumbling, slow step by step, into almost as certain a death, of fever and thirst and hunger in the wastelands, if no worse death caught him first. They told tales of this grey salt desert...

He had never before come even this far into the cold waste during all the weeks of their encampment. He was too old an

87

adventurer not to know that when people shun a place completely and talk of it in whispers and tell little half-finished, fearful stories of it over campfires, that place is better left alone. Some might have been spurred by that very reticence into investigation, but Northwest Smith had seen too many strange things in his checkered career to doubt the basis of fact behind folk-tales or care to rush in heedlessly where others had learned by experience not to tread.

The sound of battle had dwindled to a faint murmur on the evening breeze. He lifted his head painfully and stared into the gathering dark ahead with narrowed eyes the no-color of pale steel. The wind touched his keen, scarred face with a breath of utter loneliness and desolation. No man-smell of smoke or byre or farmstead tainted it, blowing clear across miles beyond miles of wastelands. Smith's nostrils quivered to that scent of unhumanity. He saw the greyness stretching before him, flat and featureless, melting into the dark. There was a sparse grass growing, and low shrub and a few stunted trees, and brackish water in deep, still pools dotted the place at far intervals. He found himself listening ...

Once in very long-ago ages, so campfire whispers had told him, a forgotten city stood here. Who dwell in it, or what, no man knew. It was a great city spreading over miles of land, rich and powerful enough to wake enmity, for a mighty foe had come at last out of the lowlands and in a series of tremendous battles razed it to the ground. What grievance they had against the dwellers in the city no one will ever know now, but it must have been dreadful, for when the last tower was laid to earth and the last stone toppled from its foundation they had sown the land with salt, so that for generations no living thing grew in all the miles of desolation. And not content with this, they had laid a curse upon the very earth wherein the city had its roots, so that even today men shun the place without understanding why.

It was very long past, that battle, and history forgot the very name of the city, and victor and vanquished alike sank together into the limbo of the forgotten. In time the salt-sown lands gained a measure of life again and the sparse vegetation that now clothed it struggled up through the barren soil. But men still shunned the place.

They said, in whispers, that there were dwellers yet in the saldands. Wolves came out by night sometimes and carried off children straying late; sometimes a new-made grave was found open and empty in the morning, and people breathed of ghouls ... late travellers had heard voices wailing from the wastes by night, and those daring hunters who ventured in search of the wild game that ran through the underbrush spoke fearfully of naked werewomen that howled in the distances. No one knew what became of the adventurous souls who travelled too far alone into the desolation of the place. It was accursed for human feet to travel, and those who dwelt there, said the legends, must be less than human.

Smith discounted much of this when he turned from the bloody shambles of that battle into the wastelands beyond. Legends grow, he knew. But a basis for the tales he did not doubt, and he glanced ruefully down at the empty holsters hanging low on his legs. He was completely unarmed, perhaps for the first time in more years than he liked to remember; for his path had run for the most part well outside the law, and such men do not go unarmed anywhere—even to bed.

Well, no help for it now. He shrugged a little, and then grimaced and caught his breath painfully, for that slash in the shoulder was deep, and blood still dripped to the ground, though not so freely as before. The wound was closing. He had lost much blood—the whole side of his leather garment was stiff with it, and the bright stain spattering behind him told of still greater losses. The pain of his shoulder stabbed at him yet, but it was being swallowed up now in a vast, heaving greyness ...

He drove his feet on stubbornly over the uneven ground, though the whole dimming landscape was wavering before him like a sea—swelling monstrously—receding into the vague distances ... The ground floated up to meet him with surprising gentleness.

He opened his eyes presently to a grey twilight, and after awhile staggered up and went on. No more blood flowed, but the shoulder was stiff and throbbing, and the wasteland heaved still like a rolling sea about him. The singing in his ears grew loud, and he was not sure whether the faint echoes of sound he heard came over grey distances or rang in his own head—long, faint howls, like wolves wailing their hunger to the stars. When he fell the second time he did not know it, and was surprised to open his eyes upon full dark with stars looking down on him and the grass tickling his cheek.

He went on. There was no great need

of it now—he was well beyond pursuit, but the dim urge to keep moving dinned in his weary brain. He was sure now that the long howls were coming to him over the waste stretches; coming nearer. By instinct his hand dropped to clutch futilely at the empty holster.

There were queer little voices going by overhead in the wind. Thin, shrill. With immense effort he slanted a glance upward and thought he could see, with the clarity of exhaustion, the long, clean lines of the wind streaming across the sky. He saw no more than that, but the small voices shrilled thinly in his ears.

Presently he was aware of motion beside him—life of some nebulous sort moving parallel to his course, invisible in the starlight. He was aware of it through the thrill of evil that prickled at the roots of his hair, pulsing from the dimness at his side—though he could see nothing. But with that clarity of inner vision he felt the vast and shadowy shape lurching formlessly through the grass at his side. He did not turn his head again, but the hackles of his neck bristled. The howls were nearing, too. He set his teeth and drove on, unevenly.

He fell for the third time by a clump of stunted trees, and lay for a while breathing heavily while long, slow waves of oblivion washed over him and receded like waves over sand. In the intervals of lucidity he knew that those howls were coming closer over the greyness of saltlands.

He went on. The illusion of that formless walker-in-the-dark still haunted him through the grass, but he was scarcely heeding it now. The howls had changed to short, sharp yaps, crisp in the starlight, and he knew that the wolves had struck his trail. Again, instinctively, his hand flashed downward toward his gun, and a spasm of pain crossed his face. Death he did not mind —he had kept pace with it too many years to fear that familiar visage—but death under fangs, unarmed ... He staggered on a httle faster, and the breath whistled through his clenched teeth.

Dark forms were circling his, slipping shadowily through the grass. They were wary, these beasts of the oudands. They did not draw near enough for him to see them save as shadows gliding among the shadows, patient and watching. He cursed thcm futilcly with his failing brcath, for he knew now that he dared not fall again. The grey waves washed upward, and he shouted something hoarse in his throat and called upon a last reservoir of strength to bear him up. The dark forms started at his voice.

So he went on, wading through oblivion that rose waist-high, shoulder-high, chin-high—and receded again before the indomitable onward drive that dared not let him rest. Something was wrong with his eyes now—the pale-steel eyes that had never failed him before—for among the dark forms he was thinking he saw white ones, slipping and gliding wraithlike in the shadow ...

For an endless while he stumbled on under the chilly stars while the earth heaved gently beneath his feet and the greyness was a sea that rose and fell in blind waves, and white figures weaved about his through the hollow dark.

Quite suddenly he knew that the end of his strength had come. He knew it surely, and in the last moment of lucidity left to him he saw a low tree outlined against the stars and staggered to it —setting his broad back against the trunk, fronting the dark watchers with lowered head and pale eyes that glared defiance. For that one moment he faced them resolutely—then the tree-trunk was sliding upward past him—the ground was rising—he gripped the sparse grass with both hands, and swore as he fell.

When he opened his eyes again he stared into a face straight out of hell. A woman's face, twisted into a diabolical smile, stooped over him—glare-eyed in the dark. White fangs slavered as she bent to his throat.

Smith choked back a strangled sound that was half oath, half prayer, and struggled to his feet. She started back with a soundless leap that set her wild hair flying, and stood staring him in the face with wide slant eyes that glared greenly from the pallor of her face. Through dark hair, her body was white as a sickle moon, half-veiled in the long, wild hair.

She glared with hungry fangs a-drip. Beyond her he sensed other forms, dark and white, circling restlessly through the shadows—and he began to understand dimly, and knew that there was no hope in hfe for him, but he spread his long legs wide and gave back glare for glare, pale-eyed and savage.

The pack circled him, dim blurs in the dark, the green glare of eyes shining alike from white shapes and black. And to his dizzied eyes it seemed that the forms were not stable; shifting from dark to light and back again with only the green-glowing eyes holding the same glare through all the changing. They were closing in now, the soft snarls rising and sharp yaps impatiently breaking through the guttural undernotes, and he saw the gleam of teeth, white under the stars.

He had no weapon, and the wasteland reeled about him and the earth heaved underfoot, but he squared his shoulders savagely and fronted them in hopeless defiance, waiting for the wave of darkness and hunger to come breaking over him in an overwhelming tide. He met the green desire of the woman's wild eyes as she stooped forward, gathering herself for the lunge, and suddenly something about the fierceness of her struck a savage chord within him, and—facing death as he was—he barked a short, wild laugh at her, and yelled into the rising wind. "Come on, were woman! Call your pack!"

She stared for the briefest instant, half-poised for leaping—while something like a spark seemed to flash between them, savageness calling to savageness across the barriers of everything alive—and suddenly she flung up her arms, the black hair whirling, and tossed back her head and bayed to the stars; a wild, long ululating yell and tossed it from voice to voice across the saltlands until the very stars shivered at the wild, exultant baying.

And as the long yell trembled into silence something inexplicable happened to Smith. Something quivered in answer within him, agonizingly, the grey oblivion he had been fighting so long swallowed him up at a gulp—and then he leaped within himself in a sudden, ecstatic rush; and while one part of him slumped to its knees and

then to its face in the grass, the living vital being that was Smith sprang free into the cold air that stung like sharp wine.

The wolf-pack rushed clamorously about him, the wild, high yells shivered delightfully along every nerve of his suddenly awakened body. And it was as if a muffling darkness had lifted from his senses, for the night opened up in all directions to his new eyes, and his nostrils caught fresh, exciting odors on the streaming wind, and in his ears a thousand tiny sounds took on sudden new clarity and meaning.

The pack that had surged so clamorously about him was a swirl of dark bodies for an instant —then in a blur and a flash they were dark no longer—rose on hind legs and cast off the darkness as they rose—and slim, white, naked werewomen swirled around him in a tangle of flashing limbs and streaming hair.

He stood half-dazed at the transition, for even the wide salt moor was no longer dark and empty, but pale grey under the stars and peopled with nebulous, unstable beings that wavered away from the white wolf-pack which ringed him, and above the clamour of wild voices that thin, shrill chattering went streaming down the wind overhead.

Out of the circling pack a white figure broke suddenly, and he felt cold arms about his neck and a cold, thin body pressing his. Then the white whirl parted violently and another figure thrust through—the fierce-eyed woman who had called him across the barriers of flesh into this half-land of her own. Her green-glaring eyes stabbed at the sister-wolf whose arms twined Smith's

They ran through strange places. The trees and the grass had taken on new shapes and meanings, and in a vague, half-realized way he was aware of curious forms looming round him...

neck, and the growl that broke from her lips was a wolfs guttural. The woman fell away from Smith's embrace, crouching at bay, as the other, with a toss of wild hair, bared her fangs and launched herself straight at the throat of the interloper. They went down in a tangle of white and tossing dark, and the pack fell still so that the only sound was the heavy breathing of the fighters and the low, choked snarls that rippled from their throats. Then over the struggle of white and black burst a sudden torrent of scarlet. Smith's nostrils flared to the odor that had a new, fascinating sweetness now—and the were-woman rose, bloody-mouthed, from the body of her rival. The green-glowing eyes met his, and a savage exultation flowing from them met as savage a delight waken-ing in his, and her keen, moon-white face broke into a smile of hellish joy.

She flung up her head again and bayed a long, triumphant cry to the stars, and the pack about her took up the yell, and Smith found his own face turned to the sky and his own throat shouting a fierce challenge to the dark.

Then they were running—jostling one another in savage play, flying over the coarse grass on feet that scarcely brushed the ground. It was like the rush of the wind, that effortless racing, as the earth flowed backward under their spurning feet and the wind streamed in their nostrils with a thousand tingling odors. The white were-woman raced at his side, her long hair flying behind her like a banner, her shoul-der brushing his.

They ran through strange places. The trees and the grass had taken on new shapes and meanings, and in a vague, half-real-ized way he was aware of curious forms looming round him — buildings, towers, walls, high turrets shining in the starlight, yet so nebulous that they did not impede their flight. He could see these shadows of a city very clearly sometimes—sometimes he ran down marble streets, and it seemed to him that his feet rang in golden sandals on the pavement and rich garments whipped behind him in the wind of his speed, and a sword clanked at his side. He thought the woman beside him fled in bright-colored sandals too, and her long skirts rippled away from her flying limbs and the streaming hair was twined with jewels—yet he knew he ran naked beside a moon-bare wolf-woman over coarse grass that rustled to his tread.

And sometimes, too, it seemed to him that he fled on four legs, not two—fleetly as the wind, thrusting a pointed muzzle into the breeze and lolling a red tongue over dripping fangs ...

Dim shapes fled from their sweeping onward rush—great, blurred, formless things; dark beings with eyes; thin wraiths wavering backward from their path. The great moor teemed with these half-seen monstrosities; fierce-eyed, some of them, breathing out menace, and evil, angry shapes that gave way reluctantly before the werepack's sweep. But they gave way. There were terrible things in that wasteland, but the most terrible of all were the werewomen, and all the dreadful, unreal beings made way at the bay of those savage voices. All this he knew intuitively. Only the thin chattering that streamed down the wind did not hush when the werevoices howled.

There were many odors on the wind that night, sharp and sweet and acrid, wild odors of wild, desolate lands and the dwellers therein. And then, quite suddenly on a vagrant breeze, lashing their nostrils like a whip—the harsh, rich, blood-tingling scent of man. Smith flung up his head to the cold stars and bayed long and shudderingly, and the wild wolf-yell rang from throat to throat through the pack until the whole band of them was shaking the very air to that savage chorus. They loped down the wind-stream, nostrils flaring to that full, rich, scent.

Smith ran at the forefront, shoulder to shoulder with the wild white creature who had fought for him. The man-smell was sweet in his nostrils, and hunger wrenched at him as the smell grew stronger and faint atavistic stirrings of anticipation rose in his memory ... Then they saw them.

A little band of hunters was crossing the moorland, crashing through the underbrush, guns on their shoulders. Blindly they walked, stumbling over hummocks that were clear to Smith's new eyes. And all about them the vague denizens of the place were gathering unseen. Great, nebulous, cloudy shapes dogged their footsteps through the grass, lurching along formlessly. Dark things with eyes flitted by, turning a hungry glare unseen upon the hunters. White shapes wavered from their path and closed in behind. The men did not see them. They must have sensed the presence of inimical beings, for now and then one would glance over his shoulder nervously, or hitch a gun forward as if he had almost seen—then lower it sheepishly and go on.

The very sight of them fired that strange hunger in Smith's new being, and again he flung back his head and yelled fiercely the long wolf-cry toward the frosty stars. At the sound of it a ripple of alarm went through the unclean, nebulous crowd that dogged the hunters' footsteps. Eyes turned toward the approaching pack, glaring angrily from bodies as unreal as smoke. But as they drew nearer the press began to melt away, the misty shapes wavering off reluctantly into the pallor of the night before the sweep of the wolves.

They skimmed over the grass, flying feet spurning the ground, and with a rush and a shout they swooped down around the hunters yelling their hunger. The men had huddled into a little knot, backs together and guns bristling outward as the werepack eddied round them. Three or four men fired at random into the circling pack, the flash and sound of it sending a wavering shudder through the pale things that had drawn back to a safe distance, watching. But the wolf-women paid no heed.

Then the leader—a tall man in a white fur cap—shouted suddenly in a voice of panic terror. "No use to fire! No use—don't you see? These aren't real wolves ..."

Smith had a fleeting realization that to human eyes they must, then, seem wolf-formed, though all about him in the pale night he saw clearly only white, naked women with flying hair circling the hunters and baying hungrily with wolf-voices as they ran.

The dark hunger was ravaging him as he paced the narrowing circle with short, nervous steps —the human bodies so near, smelling so richly of blood and flesh. Vaguely memories of that blood running sweetly eddied through his mind, and the feel of teeth meeting solidly to flesh; and beyond that a deeper hunger, inexplicably, for something he could not name. Only he felt he would never have peace again until he had sunk his teeth into the throat of that man in the white fur cap; felt blood gushing over his face ...

"Look!" shouted the man, pointing as his eyes met Smith's ravenous glare. "See—the big one with white eyes, running with the she-wolf ..." He fumbled for something inside his coat.

"The Devil himself—all the rest are green-eyed, but—white eyes—see!"

Something in the sound of his voice lashed that hunger in Smith to the breaking point. It was unbearable. A snarl choked up in his throat and he gathered himself to spring. The man must have seen the flare of it in the pale eyes meeting his, for he shouted, "God in Heaven! ..." and clawed desperately at his collar. And just as Smith's feet left the ground in a great, steel muscled

spring straight for that tempting throat, the man ripped out what he had been groping for and the starlight caught the glint of it exposed—a silver cross dangling from a broken chain.

Something blinding exploded in Smith's innermost brain. Something compounded of thunder and lightning smote him in midair. An agonized howl ripped itself from his throat as he fell back, blinded and deafened and dazed, while his brain rocked to its foundations and long shivers of dazzling force shuddered hrough the air about him.

Dimly, from a great distance, he heard the agonized howls of the werewomen, the shouts of men, the trample of shod feet on the ground. Behind his closed eyes he could still see that cross upheld, a blinding symbol from which streamers of forked lightning blazed away and the air crackled all around.

When the tumult had faded in his ears and the blaze died away and the shocked air shuddered into stillness again, he felt the touch of cold, gentle hands upon him and opened his eyes to the green glare of other eyes bending over him. He pushed her away and struggled to his feet, swaying a little as he stared round the plain. All the white werewomen were gone, save the one at his side. The huntsmen were gone. Even the misty denizens of the place were gone. Empty in the grey dimness the wasteland stretched away. Even the thin piping over-head had fallen into shocked silence. All about them the plain lay still, shuddering a little and gathering its forces again after the ordeal.

The werewoman had trotted off a little way and was beckoning to him impatiently over her shoulder. He followed, instinctively anxious to leave the spot of the disaster. Presently they were running again, shoulder to shoulder across the grass, the plain spinning away under their flying feet. The scene of that conflict fell behind them, and strength was flowing again through Smith's light-footed body, and overhead, faintly, the thin, shrill chattering began anew.

With renewed strength the old hunger flooded again through him, compellingly. He tossed up his head to test the wind, and a little whimper of eagerness rippled from his throat. An answering whine from the running woman replied to it. She tossed back her hair and sniffed the wind, hunger flaming in her eyes. So they ran through the pale night, hunter and huntress, while dim shapes wavered from their path and the earth reeled backward under their spurning feet.

It was pleasant to run so, in perfect unison, striding effortlessly with the speed of the wind, arrogantly in the knowledge of their strength, as the dreadful dwellers of the aeon-cursed moor fled from their approach and the very air shuddered when they bayed.

Again the illusion of misty towers and walls wavered in the dimness before Smith's eyes. He seemed to run down marble-paved streets, and felt again the clank of a belted sword and the ripple of rich garments, and saw the skirts of the woman beside him moulded to her limbs as she fled along with streaming, jewel-twined hair. He thought that the buildings rising so nebulously all around were growing higher as they advanced. He caught vague glimpses of arches and columns and great domed temples, and began, somehow uneasily, to sense presences in the streets, unseen but thronging.

Then simultaneously his feet seemed to strike a yielding resistance, as if he had plunged at a stride knee-deep into heavy water, and the woman beside him threw up her arms wildly in a swirl of hair and tossed back her head and screamed hideously, humanly, despairingly—the first human sound he had heard from her lips—and stumbled to her knees on the grass that was somehow a marble pavement.

Smith bent to catch her as she fell, plunging his arms into unseen resistance as he did so. He felt it suck at her as he wrenched the limp body out of those amazing, invisible wavelets that were lapping higher and higher up his legs with incredible swiftness. He swung her up clear of them, feeling the uncontrollable terror that rippled out from her body course in unbroken wavelets through his own, so he shook with nameless panic, not understanding why. The thick tide had risen mufflingly about his thighs when he turned back the way he had come and began to fight his way out of the clinging horror he could not see, the woman a weight of terror in his arms.

It seemed to be a sort of thickness in the air, indescribable, flowing about him in deepening waves that lapped up and up as if some half-solidified jelly were swiftly and relentlessly engulfing him. Yet he could see nothing but the grass underfoot, the dim, dreamlike marble pavement, the night about, the cold stars overhead. He struggled forward through the invisible thickness. It

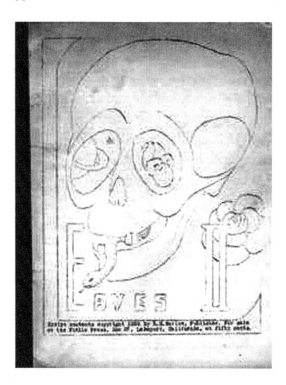

"Werewoman" was originally published in *Leaves II*, (1938), published by Robert Barlowe.

was worse than trying to run through water, with the retarded motion of nightmares. It sucked at him, draggingly, as he struggled forward through the deeps of it, stumbling, not daring to fall, the woman a dead weight in his arms.

And very slowly he won free. Very slowly he forced his way out of the clinging horror. The little lapping waves of it ceased to mount. He felt the thickness receding downward, past his knees, down about his ankles, until only his feet sucked and stumbled in invisibility, the nameless mass shuddering and quaking. And at long last he broke again, and as his feet touched the clear ground, he leaped forward wildly, like an arrow from a bow, into the delightful freedom of the open air. It felt like pure

flying after that dreadful struggle through the unseen. Muscles exulting at the release, he fled over the grass liked a winged thing while the dim building reeled away behind him and the woman stirred a little in his arms, an inconsidered weight in the joy of freedom.

Presently she whimpered a little, and he paused by a stunted tree to set her down again. She glanced round wildly. He saw from the look on her bone-white face that the danger was not yet past, and glanced round himself, seeing nothing but the dim moor with wraithlike figures wavering here and there and the stars shining down coldly. Overhead the thin shrilling went by change-lessly in the wind. All this was familiar. Yet the werewoman stood poised for instant flight, seeming unsure in just what direction danger lay, and her eyes glared panic into the dimness. He knew then that dreadful though the werepack was, a more terrible thing haunted the wasteland—invisibly, frightfully indeed to wake in the wolf-woman's eyes that staring horror. Then something touched his foot.

He leaped like the wild thing he was, for he knew that feel—even in so short a time he knew that feel. It was flowing round his foot sucking at his ankle even as he poised for flight. He seized the woman's wrist and twisted round, wrenching his foot from the invisible grip, leaping forward arrow-swift into the pale darkness. He heard her catch her breath in a sobbing gasp, eloquent of terror, as she fell into stride beside him.

So they fled, invisibility ravening at their heels. He knew, somehow, that it fol-lowed. The thick, clutching waves of it were lapping faster and faster just short of his flying feet, and he strained to the utmost, skimming over the grass like something winged and terror-stricken, the sobbing breath of the woman keeping time to his stride. What he fled he could not even guess. It had no form in any image he could conjure up. Yet he felt dimly that it was nothing alien, but rather something too horribly akin to him ... and the deadly danger he did not understand spurred on his flying feet.

The plain whirled by blurrily in their speed. Dim things with eyes fluttered away in panic as they neared, clearing a terror-stricken way for the dreadful werepeople who fled in such blind horror of something more dreadful yet.

For eternities they ran. Misty towers and walls fell away behind them. In his terror-dimmed mind it seemed to him in flashes that he was the other runner clad in rich garments and belted with the sword, running beside that other fleeing woman from another horror whose nature he did not know. He scarcely felt the ground underfoot. He ran blindly, knowing only that he must run and run until he dropped, that something far more dreadful than any death he could die was lapping hungrily at his heels, threatening him with an unnameable, incomprehensible horror— that he must run and run and run ...

And so, very slowly, the panic cleared. Very gradually sanity returned to him. He ran still, not daring to stop, for he knew the invisible hunger lapped yet not far behind—knew it surely without understanding how—but his mind had cleared enough for him to think, and his

thoughts told curious things, halfrealized things that formed images in his brain unbidden, drawn from some far source beyond his understanding. He knew, for instance, that the thing at their heels was unescapable. He knew that it would never cease its relentless pursuit, silent, invisible, remorseless, until the thick waves of it had swallowed up its quarry, and what followed that— what unimaginable horror—he somehow knew, but could not form even into thought-pictures. It was something too far outside any experience for the mind to grasp it.

The horror he felt instinctively was entirely within himself. He could see nothing pursuing him, feel nothing, hear nothing. No tremor of menace reached toward him from the following nothingness. But within him horror swelled and swelled balloon-like, a curious horror akin to something that was part of him, so it was as if he fled in terror of himself, and with no more hope of ever escaping than if indeed he fled his own shadow.

The panic had passed. He no longer ran blindly, but he knew now that he must run and run forever, hopelessly ... but his mind refused to picture the end. He thought the woman's panic had abated, too. Her breathing was evener, not the frantic gasping of that first frenzy, and he no longer felt the shaking waves of pure terror beating out from her against the ephemeral substance that was himself.

And now, as the grey landscape slid past changelessly and the thin shapes still wavered from their path and the piping went by overhead, he became conscious as he ran of a changing in the revulsion that spurred him on. There were little moments when the horror behind drew him curiously, tightening its hold on that part of his being so strangely akin to it. As a man might stare over a precipice-edge and feel the mounting urge to fling himself over, even in the face of his horror of falling, so Smith felt the strong pull of the thing that followed, if thing it might be called. Without abatement in his horror the curious desire grew to turn and face it, let it come lapping over him, steep himself in the thick invisibility—even though his whole being shuddered violently from the very thought.

Without realizing it, his pace slackened. But the woman knew, and gripped his hand fiercely, a frantic appeal rippling through him from the contact. At her touch, the pull abated for a while and he ran on in an access of revulsion, very conscious of the invisibility lapping at their heels.

While the access was at its height he felt the grip of her hand loosen a little and knew that the strange tugging at something within was reaching out for her. His hand tightened over hers and he felt the little shake she gave to free herself of that blind pull.

So they fled, the strength in each bearing the other up. Behind them relentlessly the Something followed. Twice a forward lapping wave of it brushed Smith's heel. And stronger and stronger grew the blind urge within him to turn, to plunge into the heavy flow of what followed, to steep himself in invisibility until—until— He could form no picture of that ultimate, but each time he reached the point of picturing

it a shudder went over him and blankness clouded his mind.

And ever within him that thing akin to the Follower strengthened and grew, a blind urge from his innermost being. It grew so strong that only the grip of the werewoman's hand held him from turning, and the plain faded from about him like a grey dream and he ran through a curving void —a void that he somehow knew was bending back upon itself so that he must eventually, if he ran on, come round behind his pursuer and overtake it, wade head-on into the thick deeps of invisibility ... yet he dared not slacken his running, for then it would catch him from behind. So he spun in the treadmill, terror ahead, terror behind, with no choice but to run and no hope for all his running.

When he saw the plain at all it was in dim flashes, unaccountably blurred and not always at the correct angles. It tilted without reason. Once he saw a dark pool of water slanting before him like a door, and once a whole section of landscape hung mirage-like above his head. Sometimes he panted up steep inclines, sometimes he skimmed fleedy down steeper slopes—yet he knew the plain in reality lay flat and featureless from edge to edge.

And now, though he had long ago left those misty towers and walls far behind, he began to be aware that his flight had somehow twisted and they loomed once more, shadowily, overhead. With a sickening sense of futility he fled again down the dream-vague marble pavements between rows of cloudy palaces.

Through all these dizzy metamorphoses the pursuer flowed relentlessly behind, lapping at his heels when he slowed. He began to realize, very dimly, that it might have overtaken him with ease, but that he was being spurred on thus for some vast, cloudy purpose—perhaps so that he might complete the circle he was so vaguely aware of and plunge of his own effort headlong into the very thing from which he fled. But he was not fleeing now, he was being driven.

The dim shapes of buildings reeled past. The woman running at his side had become something cloudy and vague too, a panting presence flying from the same peril—into the same peril—but unreal as a dream. He felt himself unreal too, a phantom fleeing hand-in-hand with another phantom through the streets of a phantom city. And all reality was melting away save the unreal, invisible thing that pursued him, and only it had reality while everything else faded to shapes of nothingness. Like driven ghosts they fled.

And as reality melted about them, the shadowy city took firmer shape. In the reversal everything real became cloudy, grass and trees and pools dimming like some forgotten dream, while the unstable outlines of the towers loomed up more and more clearly in the pale dark, colors flushing them as if reviving blood ran through the stones. Now the city stood firm and actual around them, and vague trees thrust themselves mistily through unbroken masonry, shadows of grass waved over firm marble pavements. Superimposed upon the unreal, the real world seemed vague as a mirage.

It was a curious architecture that rose around them now, so old and so forgotten that the very shapes of it were fantastic to Smith's eyes. Men in silk and steel moved down the streets, wading to their greave-clad knees in shadowy grass they did not seem to see. Women, too, brushed by in mail as fine-linked and shining as gowns of silver tissue, belted with swords like the men. Their faces were set in a strained stare, and though they hurried they gave an impression of aimlessness, as if moved by some outer compulsion they did not understand.

And through the hurrying crowd, past the strange-colored towers, over the grass-shadowed streets, werewoman and wolfman fled like the shadows they had become, pale wraiths blowing through the crowds unseen, the invisible follower lapping at their feet when they faltered. That force within which had urged them to turn and meet the pursuer now commanded them irresistibly to flee—to flee toward that same ending, for they knew now that they ran toward what they fled, roundaboutly; yet dared not stop running for deadly fear of what flowed along behind.

Yet in the end they did turn. The werewoman ran now in blind submission, all the strength dissolved that at first had carried her on. She was like a ghost blowing along on a gale, unresisting, unquestioning, hopeless. But in Smith a stouter spirit dwelt. And something strong and insistent was urging him to turn—an insistence that had no relation to the other urge to wait. It may have been a very human revolt against being driven, it may have been a deeply ingrained dislike of running from anything, or of allowing death to overtake him from behind. It had been bred in him to face danger when he could not escape it, and the old urge that every fighting thing knows— even a cornered rat will turn—drove him at last to face what followed him and die resisting—not in flight. For he felt that the end must be very near now. Some instinct stronger than the force that harried them told that.

And so, ignoring the armored crowd that eddied round them, he gripped the werewoman's wrist hard and slackened his speed, fighting against the urge that would have driven him on, choking down the panic that rose involuntarily as he waited for the thick waves to begin their surging round his feet. Presently he saw the shadow of a tree leaning through the smooth stone of a building, and instinctively he chose that misty thing he knew to be real for a bulwark to set his back against, rather than the unreal wall that looked so solid to his eyes. He braced his shoulders, holding a firm grip on the woman's wrist as she struggled and whimpered and moaned in her wolf-voice, straining to break the hold and run on. About, the mail-clad crowd hurried by heedlessly.

And very soon he felt it—the lapping wavelets touching his toes. He shuddered through all his unreal body at the feel, but he stood steady, gripping the struggling wolf-woman in a resolute hold, feeling the thick waves flowing around his feet, creeping up to his ankles, lapping higher and higher round his legs.

For a while he stood at bay, feeling terror choke up and up in his throat as the waves rose round him, scarcely heeding the woman's struggles to be free. And then a further rebellion began to stir. If die he must, let it be neither in headlong flight nor in dazed and terrified quiescence, but violently, fighting against it, taking some toll, if he could, to pay for the life he was to lose. He gasped a deep breath and plunged forward into the quaking, unseen mass that had risen almost to his waist. Behind him at arm's length the werewoman stumbled unwillingly.

He lurched forward. Very swiftly the unseen rose about him, until arms and shoulders were muffled in thickness, until the heavy invisibility brushed his chin, his closed mouth, sealed his nostrils ... closed over his head.

Through the clear deeps he forged on, moving like a man in a nightmare of retarded motion. Every step was an immense effort against that flow, dragged through resisting depths of jelly-like nothingness. He had all but forgotten the woman he dragged along behind. He had wholly forgotten the colored city and the shining, armored people hurrying past. Blinded to everything but the deep-rooted instinct to keep moving, he forced his slow way onward against the flow. And indescribably he felt it begin to permeate him, seeping in slowly through the atoms of his ephemeral being. He felt it, and felt a curious change coming over him by degrees, yet could not define it or understand what was happening. Something urged him fiercely to go on, to struggle ahead, not to surrender—and so he fought, his mind whirling and the strange stuff of the thing that engulfed him soaking slowly through his being.

Presently the invisibility took on a faint body, a sort of clear opaqueness, so that the things outside were streaked and blurred a little and the splendid dream city with its steel-robed throngs wavered through the walls of what had swallowed him up. Everything was shaking and blurring and somehow changing. Even his body no longer obeyed him completely, as if it trembled on the verge of transition into something different and unknown. Only the driving instinct to fight on held clear in his dazed mind. He struggled forward.

And now the towered city was fading again, its mailed people losing their outlines and melting into the greyness. But the fading was not a reversal the shadow-grass and trees grew more shadowy still. It was as if by successive steps he was leaving all matter behind. Reality had faded almost to nothing, even the cloudy unreality of the city was going now, and nothing but a grey blankness remained, a blankness through which he forged stubbornly against the all-engulfing flow that steeped him in nothingness.

Sometimes in flashes he ceased to exist—joined the grey nothing as part of it. The sensation was not that of unconsciousness. Somehow utter nirvana swallowed him up and freed him again, and between the moments of blank he fought on, feeling the transition of his body taking place very slowly, very surely, into something that even now he could not understand.

For grey eternities he struggled ahead through the clogging resistance, through darknesses of nonexistence, through flashes of near-normality, feeling somehow that the path led in wild loops and whorls through spaces without name. His time-sense had stopped. He could hear and see nothing, he could feel nothing but the immense effort of dragging his limbs through the stuff that enfolded him, and the effort was so great that he welcomed those spaces of blankness when he did not exist even as an unconsciousness. Yet stubbornly, unceasingly, the blind instinct drove him on.

There was a while when the flashes of nonexistence crowded closer and closer, and the metamorphosis of his body was all but complete, and only during brief winks of consciousness did he realize himself as an independent being. Then in some unaccountable way the tension slackened. For a long moment without interludes he knew himself a real being struggling upstream through invisibility and dragging a half-fainting woman by the wrist. The clarity of it startled him. For a while he could not understand—then it dawned upon him that his head and shoulders were free—free! What had happened he could not imagine, but he was free of it.

The hideousness grey nothingness had gone—he looked out over a plain dotted with low trees and low, white, columned villas like no architecture he had ever seen before. A little way ahead a stone slab no higher than himself leaned against a great boulder in a hollow fringed with trees. Upon the slab an indescribable symbol was incised. It was like no symbol of any writing he had ever seen before. It was so different from all the written characters men make that it scarcely seemed akin to writing at all, nor traced by any human hand. Yet there was a curious familiarity about it, that did not even puzzle him. He accepted it without question. He was somehow akin to it.

And between him and the engraved slab the air writhed and undulated. Streamers of invisibility flowed toward him, mounting as they flowed. He struggled forward, exultation surging within him. For—he knew, now. And as he advanced the thick resistance fell away from him, sliding down his shoulders, ebbing lower and lower about his struggling body. He knew that whatever the invisibility was, its origin lay in that symbol on the stone. From that it flowed. Half-visibly, he could see it. And toward that stone he made his way, a dim purpose forming in his brain.

He heard a little gasp and quickened breathing behind him, and turned his head to see the werewoman, moon-white in the undulating, almost-visible flow, staring about with wakened eyes and incomprehension clouding her face. He saw that she did not remember anything of what had happened. Her green-glowing eyes were empty as if they had just opened from deep slumber.

He forged on swiftly now through the waves that lapped futilely around his waist. He had won. Against what he did not yet know, nor from what cloudy terror he had saved himself and her, but he was not afraid now. He knew what he must do, and he struggled on eagerly toward the slab.

He was still waist-deep in the resisting flow when he reached it, and for a dizzy instant he thought he could not stop; that he must wade on into the very substance of that unnameable carving out of which came the engulfing nothingness. But with an effort he wrenched round and waded cross-stream, and after a while of desperate struggle he broke free into the open air.

It was like a cessation of gravity. In the release from that dragging weight he felt he must scarcely be touching the ground, but there was no time now to exult in his freedom. He turned purposefully toward the slab.

The werewoman was just floundering clear of the stream when she saw what he intended, and she flung up her hands with a shriek of protest that startled Smith into a sidewise leap, as if some new terror were coming upon him. Then he saw what it was and gave her an amazed stare as he turned again to the stone, lifting his arms to grapple with it. She reeled forward and seized him in a cold, desperate embrace, dragging backward with all her might. Smith glared at her and shook his shoulders impatiently. He had felt the rock give a little. But when she saw that, she screamed again piercingly, and her arms twined like snakes as she struggled to drag him away.

She was very strong. He paused to unwind the fierce clasp and she fought savagely to prevent it. He needed all his strength to break her grip, and he pushed her from him then with a heavy shove that sent her reeling. The pale eyes followed her, puzzling why, though she had fled in such a frenzy of terror from what flowed out of the stone, she still strove to prevent him from destroying it. For he was quite sure that if the slab were broken and the symbol destroyed that stream would cease to flow. He could not understand her. He shook his shoulders impatiently and turned again to the stone.

This time she was on him with an animal spring, snarling low in her throat and clawing with frantic hands. Her fangs snapped just clear of his throat. Smith wrenched free with a great effort, for she was steel-strong and very desperate, and gripped her by the shoulder, swinging her away.

Then he set his teeth and drove a heavy fist into her face, smashing against the fangs. She yelped, short and sharply, and collapsed under his hand, sinking to the grass in a huddle of whiteness and wild black hair.

He turned to the stone again. This time he got a firm grip on it, braced his legs wide, heaved. And he felt it give. He heaved again. And very slowly, very painfully, he uprooted its base from the bed where for ages it must have lain. Rock ground protestingly against rock. One edge rose a little, then settled. And the slab tilted. He heaved again, and very deliberately he felt it slipping from his hands. He stood back, breathing heavily, and watched.

Majestically, the great slab tottered. The stream flowing invisibly from its incised symbol twisted in a streaked path through the air, long whorls of opacity blurring the landscape beyond. Smith thought he felt a stirring in the air, a shiver as of warning. All the white villas dimly seen through the dark wavered a little before his eyes, and something hummed through the air like a thin, high wailing too sharp to be heard save as a pain to the ears. The chattering overhead quickened suddenly. All this in the slow instant while the slab tottered.

Then it fell. Deliberately slow, it leaned outward and down. It struck the ground with a rush and a splintering crash. He saw the long cracks appear miraculously upon its

surface as the great fantastic symbol broke into fragments. The opacity that had flowed outward from it writhed like a dragon in pain, flung itself high-arching into the shivering air—and ceased. In that moment of cessation the world collapsed around him. A mighty wind swooped down in a deafening roar, blurring the landscape. He thought he saw the white villas melting like dreams, and he knew the werewoman on the grass must have recovered consciousness, for he heard a wolf-yell of utter agony from behind him. Then the great wind blotted out all other things, and he was whirling through space in a dizzy flight.

In that flight understanding overtook him. In a burst of illumination he knew quite suddenly what had happened and what would happen now—realized without surprise, as if he had always known it, that the denizens of this wasteland had dwelt here under the protection of that mighty curse laid upon the land in the long-past century when the city fell. And he realized that it must have been a very powerful curse, laid down by skill and knowledge that has long since vanished even from the legends of man, for in all the ages since, this accursed moor had been safe haven for all the half-real beings that haunt mankind, akin to the evil that lay like a blanket over the moor.

And he knew that the curse had its origin in the nameless symbol which some sorcerer of forgotten times had inscribed upon the stone, a writing from some language which can have no faintest-kinship with man. He knew that the force flowing out from it was a force of utter evil, spreading like a river over the whole salt waste. The stream of it lapped to and fro in changing courses over the land, and when it neared some dweller of the place the evil that burnt for a life-force in that dweller acted as a magnet to the pure evil which was the stream. So, evil answering to evil, the two fused into one, the unfortunate dweller swallowed up into a nirvana of nonexistence in the heart of that slow-flowing stream.

It must have worked strange changes in them. That city whose shapes of shadow still haunted the place assumed reality, taking on substance and becoming more and more actual as the reality of the captive waned and melted into the power of the stream.

He thought, remembering those hurrying throngs with their strained, pale faces, that the spirits of the people who had died in the lost city must be bound tenuously to the spot of their death. He remembered that young, richly garmented warrior he had been one with in fleeting moments, running golden-sandaled through the streets of the forgotten city in a panic of terror from something too long past to be remembered—the jeweled woman in her colored sandals and rippling robes running at his side—and wondered in the space of a second what their story had been so many ages ago. He thought that curse must somehow have included the dwellers in the city, chaining them in earthbound misery for centuries. But of this he was not sure.

Much of all this was not clear to him, and more he realized without understanding, but he knew that the instinct which guided him to turn upstream had not been a false one—that something human and alien in him had been a talisman to lead his staggering feet back toward the source of his destroyer. And he knew that with the breaking up of the symbol that was a curse, the curse ceased to be, and the warm,

(Continued on page 120)

C.L. (Catherine Lucille) Moore (1911-1987) developed two significant series characters in *Weird Tales* magazine — Northwest Smith, a space pilot and smuggler, who predated Han Solo in the *Star Wars* series by decades; and Jirel of Joiry, an early example of the swordswoman/warrior.

Her stories appeared in *Weird Tales, Astounding Stories, Fantasy Magazine, Scienti-Snaps, Famous Fantastic Mysteries, The Magazine of Fantasy and Science Fiction,* and *Alfred Hitchcock's Mystery Magazine.*

In 1946, Moore married Henry Kuttner, another prominent author of science fiction. She taught a writing course at the University of Southern California, and briefly wrote television scripts at Warner Brothers. After her retirement, she remained active with science fiction fandom until her death.

The
Tree-Man

by HENRY S. WHITEHEAD

MY FIRST sight of Fabricius, the tree-man, was within a week of my first arrival on the island of Santa Cruz not long after the United States had purchased the Danish West Indies and officially renamed its new colony the Virgin Islands of the United States.

My ship came into Frederiksted harbour on the west coast of the island just at dusk and I saw for the first time a half-moon of white sand beach with the charming little town in its middle. In the midst of the bustle incident to anchoring in the roadstead, there came over the side an upstanding gentleman in a glistening white drill uniform who came up to me, bowed in a manner to commend itself to kings, and said:

"I am honoured to welcome you to Santa Cruz, Mr. Canevin. I am Director Despard of the Police Department. The police boat is at your disposal when you are ready to go ashore. May I see to your luggage?"

This was a welcome indeed. I was nearly knocked off my feet by such an unexpected reception. I thanked Director Despard and before many minutes my trunks were overside, my luggage bestowed in the police boat waiting at the foot of the ladder-gangway, and I was seated beside him in the boat's sternsheets, he holding the tiller-ropes while four coal-black convicts rowed us ashore with lusty pulls at their long sweeps.

Through the lowering dusk as we approached the landing I observed that the wharf was crowded with black people. Behind these stood half a dozen knots of white people, conversing together. A long row of cars stood against the background of waterfront buildings. I remarked to the Police Director:

"Isn't it unusual for so many persons to be on the docks for the arrival of a vessel, Mr. Director?"

"It is not usual," replied the dignified gentleman beside me. "It is for you, Mr. Canevin."

"For me?" said I. "Extraordinary! What—for me? Certainly,—my dear sir,—certainly not for me. Why, it's…"

Mr. Despard turned about and smiled at me.

"You are Captain McMillin's great-nephew, you know, Mr. Canevin."

So that was it. My great-uncle, one of my Scots kinsfolk, my great-uncle who had died many years before I had seen the light of day, my grandfather's oldest brother, the one who had been in the British Army and later a planter here on Santa Cruz. He had been the very last person I should have thought of, and now—

The police boat landed smartly at the concrete jetty. Mr. Despard and I landed, and in the lowering dusk I could not help noticing the quietly-expressed but very genuine interest of the thousand or more negroes who thronged the wharf as they courteously parted a way for us while we proceeded towards the groups of white people, thronging forward now with an unanimous and unmistakable greeting shining from dozens of kindly faces.

I will pass over the rest of that first evening ashore. At the end of it and all its lavish hospitality I found myself comfortably installed in a small private hotel pending the final preparations to my own hired residence. I found every estate-house on Santa Cruz open to me. Hospitalities were showered upon me to the point of embarrassment, kindnesses galore, considerate and timely bits of information, help of every imaginable kind. I learned in this process

This version of "Tree-Man" was published in Leaves II, an "amateur" publication from Robert Barlow, a noted horror fan and friend of H.P. Lovecraft. (See 'A Tale of Two Stories' by Dave Goudsward in this issue)

When August Derleth reprinted "Tree Man," this significantly revised version was published, not the original text from Weird Tales *magazine.*

much about my late great-uncle, all of which information was new to me, and it was not long after my arrival when it was arranged for me to visit his estate, Great Fountain.

I went with Hans Grumbach, in his Ford car, a bumpy journey of more than three hours up hills and through ravines and along precipitous trails on old roads incredibly roundabout and primitive.

All the way Hans Grumbach talked about this section of the island, now rarely visited. Here, up to ten years before, Grumbach had lived as the last of a long line of estate-managers which the old place had had in residence since the day, in 1879, when my Scottish relatives had sold their Santa Crucian holdings. It was now the property of the largest of the local sugar-growing corporations, known as the Copenhagen Concern. Because of its inaccessibility cultivation on it had finally been abandoned and Hans Grumbach had come to live in Frederiksted, married the daughter of a respectable *creole* family, and settled down to keeping store on one of the town's side streets.

But, it came out, Grumbach had wanted for all those ten years, to go back to the northern hills. This trip to the old place stimulated his loquacity. He sang its praises: the beauty of its configuration, its magnificent views and vistas, the amazing fertility of its soil.

We arrived at last. All about us the vegetation had grown to be ideally tropical, the "tropical" of old-fashioned pictures on calendars! The soil appeared to be rich, blackish "bottomland."

The old estate was in a sad state of rack and ruin. We walked over a good part of it under the convoy of the courteous black caretaker, and looked out over its rolling domain from various angles and coigns of vantage. The Negro village was half tumbled-down. The cabins remaining were all out of repair. The characteristic quick tropical inroads upon land "turned out" of active cultivation were everywhere apparent. The ancient Great House was entirely gone. The farm buildings, though built of sound stone and mortar, were terribly dilapidated.

On that visit to Great Fountain I had my first experience of the "grapevine" method of communication among Africans. I had been perhaps four days on the island, and it is reasonably certain that none of these people had ever so much as heard of me before; these obscure village negroes cut off here in the hills from others the nearest of whom lived miles away. Yet, we had hardly come within a stone's throw of the remains of the village before we were surrounded by the total population, of perhaps twenty adults, and at least as many children of all ages.

As one would expect, these blacks were of very crude appearance; not only "country negroes" but that in an exaggerated form. Negroes in the West Indies have some tendency to live on the land where they originated, and as it happened most of these negroes had been born up here and several generations of their forebears before them.

We had brought our lunch along, and this Hans Grumbach and I ate sitting in the Ford under the shade of a grove of magnificent old mahogany trees, and afterwards Grumbach took me up along a ravine to see the "fountain" from which the old estate had originally derived its title.

The "fountain" itself was a delicate natural waterfall, streaming thinly over the edge of a high rock. It was when we were coming back, by a slightly different route, for Grumbach wanted me to take in everything possible, that I saw the tree-man.

He stood, a youngish, coal-black Negro, of about twenty-five years, scantily dressed in a tattered shirt and a sketchy pair of trousers, about ten yards away from the field-path we were following and from which a clear view of a portion of the estate was obtained, and beside him, towering over him, was a magnificent coconut-palm. The Negro stood motionless. I thought, in fact, that he had gone asleep standing there, both arms clasped about the tree's smooth, elegant trunk, the right side of his face pressed against it.

He was not, however, asleep, because I looked back at him and his eyes—rather intelligent eyes, they seemed to me—were wide open, although to my surprise he had not changed his position, nor even the direction of his gaze, to glance at us; and, I was quite sure, he had not been in that village group when we had stood among them just before our lunch.

Grumbach did not speak to him, as he had done to every other Negro we had seen. Indeed, I observed that his face looked a trifle—well, apprehensive; and I thought he very slightly quickened his pace. I stepped nearer to him as we walked past the man and the tree, and then I noticed that his lips were moving, and when I came closer I observed that he was muttering to himself. I said, very quietly, almost in his ear:

"What's the matter with that fellow, Grumbach?"

Grumbach glanced at me out of the corner of his eye, and my impression that he was disturbed grew upon me.

"He's listening!" was all that I got out of Grumbach. I supposed, of course, that there was something odd about the fellow; perhaps he was slightly demented and might be an annoyance; and I supposed that Grumbach meant to convey that the young fellow was "listening" for our possible comment upon him and his strange behaviour. Later, after we had said good-bye to the courteous caretaker and he had seen us off down the first hillside road, with its many ruts, I brought up the subject of the young black fellow at the tree.

"You mentioned that he was listening," said I, "so I dropped the matter, but, why does he do that, Grumbach—I mean, why does he stand against the tree in that unusual manner? Why, he didn't even gee his eyes to look at us, and that surprised me. They don't have visitors up here every day, I understand."

"He was listening—*to his tree!*" said Hans Grumbach, as though reluctantly. "*That* was what I meant, Mr. Canevin." And he drew my attention to an extraordinarily picturesque ruined windmill, the kind once used for the grinding of cane in the old days of "muscovado" sugar, which dominated a cone-like hillside off to our left as we bumped over the road. It was not until months later, when I had gained the confidence of Hans Grumbach, that that individual gave me any further enlightenment on the subject of the man and his tree.

Then I learned that, along with his nostalgia for the life of an agriculturist—an incurable matter with some persons I have found—there was mixed in with his feelings about the Great Fountain estate a kind of inconsistent thankfulness that he was no longer stationed there! This inconsistency, this being dragged sentimentally in two opposite directions, rather intrigued me. I saw something of Grumbach and got rather well acquainted with him as the months passed that first year of my residence. Bit by bit, in his reluctant manner of speech, it came out.

To put the whole picture of his mind on this subject together, I got the idea that Grumbach, while always suffering from a faint nostalgia for his deep-country residence and the joys of tilling the soil, felt, somehow, *safe* here in the town. If he chafed, mildly, at the restrictions of town life and his storekeeping, there was yet the certainty that "something"—a vague matter at first, as it came out—was not always hanging over him; something connected with a lingering fear.

The negroes, it appeared—this came to me very gradually, of course—up there at Great Fountain, were not, quite, like the rest of the island's black population; in the two towns; out on the many sugar-estates; even those residues of village communities which continued to live, in that mild, beneficent climate, on "turned-out" estate land because there was no one sufficiently interested to eject these squatters. No— the Great Fountain village was, somehow, at least in Hans Grumbach's dark hints, dif-

ferent; *sui generis*; a peculiar people.

They were, to begin with, almost purely of Dahomeyan stock. These Dahomeyans had drifted "down the islands" from Hayti, beginning soon after the revolt against France in the early Nineteenth Century. They were tall, very black, extremely clannish blacks. And just as the Loromantyn slaves in British Jamaica had brought to the West Indies their Obay-i-, or herb-magic, so, it seemed, had the Dahomeyans carried with them from Guinea their vodu, which properly defined, means the practices accompanying the worship of "the Snake."

This worship, grown into a vast localised *cultus* in unfettered Hayti and in the Guiana hinterlands down in South America, is very imperfectly understood. But its accompaniments, all the charms, *ouangas*, philtres, potions, talismans, amulets, "doctoring" and whatnot, have spread all through the West India islands, and these are thoroughly established in highly developed and widely variant forms. Hayti is its West Indian home, of course. But down in French Martinique its extent and intensity is a fair rival to the Haytian supremacy. It is rife on Dominica, Guadeloupe, even on British Montserrat. Indeed, one might name every island from Cuba to Trinidad, and, allowing for the variations, the local preferences, and all such matters, one might say, and truly, that the *vodu*, generically described by the blacks themselves as "obi," is very thoroughly established.

According to Grumbach, the handful of villagers at Great Fountain was very deeply involved in this sort of thing.

"The Tree-Man" was originally published in *Weird Tales,* **February-March 1934; Popular Fiction Publishing Co.; Chicago**

Left to themselves as they had been for many years, forming a little, self-sustaining community of nearly pure-blooded Dahomeyans, they had, it seemed, reverted very nearly to their African type; and this, Grumbach alleged, was the fact despite their easy kindliness, their use of "English," and the various other outward appearances which caused them to seem not greatly different from other "country negroes" on this island of Santa Cruz.

Grumbach had known Silvio Fabricius since he had been a pick'ny on the estate. He knew, so far as his limited under-standing of black people's magic extended, all about Silvio. He had been estate-manager at the time the boy had begun his attentions to the great coconut palm. He had heard and seen what he called the "stupidness" which had attended the setting apart of this neophyte. There had been three days—and nights; particularly the nights—when not a single plantation-hand would do a piece of work for any consideration. It was, as Grumbach bitterly remembered it all, "the crop season." His employers, not sensing, businessmen as they were, any underlying reason for no work done when they needed the cane from Great Fountain for their grinding-mill, had been hard on him. They had, in Santa Crucian phraseology, "pressed him" for cane deliveries. And there, in his village, quite utterly ignoring his authority as estate-manager, those blacks had danced and pounded drums, and burned flares, and weaved back and forth in their interminable ceremonies—"stupidness"—for three strategic days and nights, over something which had Silvio Fabricius, then a rising pick'ny of twelve or thirteen, as its apparent centre and underlying cause. It was no wonder that Hans Grumbach raved and probably swore mightily and threatened the estate-hands.

But his anger and annoyance, the threats and cajolings, the offers of "snaps" of rum, and pay for piece-work; all these efforts to get his ripe cane cut and delivered; had come to nothing. The carts stood empty. The mules gravely ate the long guinea-grass. The canetops waved in the soft breath of the North-East Trade Wind, while those three days stretched themselves out to their conclusion.

This conclusion, which was ceremonial, took place in the daytime, about ten o'clock in the morning of the fourth day.

After that, which was a very brief and apparently. meaningless matter indeed, the hands sheepishly resumed the driving of their mule-carts and the swinging of their cane-bills, and once more the Fountain cane travelled slowly down the rutted hill road towards the factory below. On that morning, before resuming their work, the whole village had accompanied young Silvio Fabricius in silence as he walked ahead of them up towards the source of the perennial stream, stepped out into the field, and clasped his arms about a young, but tall and promising coconut palm which stood there as though accidentally in solitary towering grandeur. There the villagers had left the little black boy when they turned away and filed slowly and silently back to the village and to their interrupted labour.

And there, beside his tree, Grumbach said, Silvio Fabricius had stood ever since, only occasionally coming in to the village and then at any hour of the day or night, apparently "reporting" something to the oldest inhabitant, a gnarled, ancient grandfather with pure white wool. After such a brief visit Fabricius would at once, and with an unshaken gravity, return to his tree. Food, said Grumbach, was always carried out to him from the village. He toiled not, neither spun! There, day and night, under the blazing sun, through showers and drenching downpours, erect, apparently unsleeping—unless he slept standing up against his tree as Grumbach suspected— stood Silvio Fabricius, and there he had stood, except when he climbed the tree to trim out the "cloth" or chase out a rat intent on nesting up there, or to gather the coconuts, for eleven years.

The coconuts, it seemed, were his perquisite. They were, Grumbach said, absolutely tabu to anybody else. It was over the question of some green coconuts from this superior tree that Grumbach himself, with all his authority as estate-manager behind his demand, had come to grips with Silvio Fabricius; or, to be more precise, with the entire estate-village.

I never succeeded in getting this story in detail from Grumbach, who was plainly reluctant to tell it. It reflected, you see, upon him; his authority as estate-manager, his pride, were here heavily involved. But, as I gathered it, his houseman, sent to that particular tree for a basket of green coconuts—Grumbach was entertaining some friends and wanted the coconut-water and jelly to put in a Danish concoction based on Holland gin—had returned half an hour late, delivered the coconuts, and later, it came out that he had gone *down* the hill to a neighbouring estate for the nuts. Taken to task for this duplicity, the house-man had balked, "gone stupid" over the affair, and upon the dispute which followed the village itself had joined in. The conclusion, as Grumbach gathered it, to his great mystification, was that the coconut tree "belonged to" young Silvio Fabricius, was *tabu*, and that the village was solid against him on the issue. He, the manager, with control of everything, could not get coconuts from the best tree on the estate! This, attributed to the usual black "stupidness" had rankled. It also more or less accounted for Grumbach's attitude towards Silvio Fabricius, an attitude which I myself had witnessed. That his "fear" of this young negro went deeper than that, I sensed, however. I was, later, to see that suspicion justified.

For a long time I had no occasion to revisit Great Fountain. But six years later, while in the States during the summer, I made the acquaintance of a man named Carrington who wanted to know "all about the Virgin Islands" with a view to investing some money there in a proposal to grow pineapples on a large scale. I talked with Mr. Carrington at some length, and in the course of our discussions it occurred to me that Great Fountain estate would be virtually ideal for his purpose. Here was a very considerable acreage of rich land: the Copenhagen Company would probably rent it out for a period of ten years for a very reasonable price since it was bringing them in nothing. I spread before Carrington these advantages, and he travelled down on the ship with me that autumn to make an investigation in person.

Carrington, a trained fruit-grower, spent a day with me on the estate, and thereafter with characteristic American energy started in to put his plan into practice. A lease was easily secured, the village was repaired and the fallen stone cabins rebuilt, and within a few weeks cultivating machinery of the most modern type began to arrive on the Frederik-sted wharf.

After a considerable consultation with Hans Grumbach, to whose lamentations over the restrictions of town-life I had been listening for years, I recommended him to Mr. Carrington as manager of the labourers, and Hans, after going over the matter with his good wife and coming to an amicable understanding, went back to Great Fountain where a manager's house had been thrown up for him on the foundation of one of the ruined buildings. At Carrington's direction, Grumbach set the estate labourers at work on the job of repairing the roads; and, as the village cabins went up, one after another, labourers, enticed by the prospect of good wages, filled them up and ancient Great Fountain became once more a busy scene of industry.

During these preparatory works I spent a good deal of time on the estate because I was naturally interested in Joseph Carrington's venture being a success. I had, indeed, put several thousand dollars into it myself, not solely because it looked like a good investment, but in part for sentimental reasons connected with my great-uncle. Being by then thoroughly familiar with the odd native speech, I made it a point to visit the village and talk at length with the "people." They were courteous to me, markedly so; deferential would be a better word to describe their attitude. This, of course, was wholly due to the family connection. Only a very few of them, and those the oldest, had any personal recollection of Captain McMillin, but his memory was decidedly green among them. The old gentleman had been greatly beloved by the negroes of the island.

In the course of my reading I had run across the peculiar affair of a "tree-man." I understood, therefore, the status of Silvio Fabricius in that queer little black community; why he had been "devoted" to the tree; what were the underlying reasons for that strange sacrifice.

It was, on the part of that handful of

nearly pure-blooded Dahomeyan villagers there at my great-uncle's old place, a revival of a custom probably as old as African civilisation. For—the African *has* a civilisation. He is at a vast disadvantage when among Caucasians, competing, as he necessarily must, with Caucasian "cultures." His native problems are entirely different, utterly diverse, from the white man's. The African's whole history among us Caucasians is a history of more or less successful adaptation. Place an average American businessman in the heart of "uncivilised" Africa, in the Liberian hinterland, for example, and what will he do—how survive? The answer is simple. He will perish miserably, confronted with the black jungle night, the venomous reptilian and insect-life, the attacks of wild beasts, the basic problems of how to feed and warm himself—for even this last is an African problem. I know. I have been on *safari* in Uganda, in British East Africa, in Somali-land. I speak from experience.

Africans, supposedly static in cultural matters, have solved all these problems. And, very prominent among these, especially as it concerns the agricultural peoples; for there are, perhaps, as many black nations, kindreds, peoples, tongues, as there are Caucasian; is, of course, the question of weather.

Hence, the "tree-man."

Set apart with ceremonies which were ancient when Hammurabi sat on his throne in Babylon, a young boy is dedicated to a forest tree. Thereafter he spends his life beside that tree, cares for it, tends it, listens to it; becomes "the-brother-of-the-tree" in time. He is truly "set apart." To the tree he devotes his entire life, dying at last beside it, in its shade. And—this is African "culture" if you will; a culture of which we Caucasians get, perhaps, the faint reactions in the (to us) meaningless jumble of negro superstition which we sense all about us; the "stupidity" of the West Indies; faint, incomprehensible reflections of a system as practical, as dogmatic, as utilitarian, as the now well-nigh universal system of synthetic exercise for the tired businessman which goes by the name of golf!

These negroes at Great Fountain were, primarily, agriculturists. They had the use of the soil bred deeply in their blood and bones. That, indeed, is why the canny French brought their Hispaniola slaves from Dahomey. Left to themselves at the old estate in the north central hills of Santa Cruz the little community rapidly reverted to their African ways. They tilled the soil, sporadically, it is true, yet they tilled it. They needed a weather prognosticator. There are sudden storms in summer throughout the vast sweep of the West India Islands, devastating storms, hurricanes indeed; long, wasting periods of drought. They needed a tree-man up there. They set apart Silvio Fabricius.

That fact made the young fellow what a white man would call "scared." Not for nothing had they danced and performed their "stupid" rites those three long days and nights to the detriment of Hans Grumbach's deliveries. No. Silvio Fabricius, from the moment he had clasped his arms about that growing coconut-palm, was as much a person "set apart," dedicated, as any white man's pundit, priest, or yogi.

Hence the various *tabus* which, like the case of the green coconuts, had puzzled Hans Grumbach. He must never take his attention away from the tree. There, beside it, he was consecrated to live and to die. When he departed from his "brother" the tree, it was only for the purpose of reporting something which the tribe should know; something, that is, which his brother the tree had told him! There would be drenching rain the second day following. A plague of small green flies would, the third day later, come to annoy the animals. The banana grove must be propped forthwith. Otherwise, a high wind, two days hence, would nullify all the work of its planting and care.

Such were the messages that Silvio Fabricius, austere, introspective, unnoticing, his mind fully preoccupied with his brotherhood to the tree, brought to his tribe; proceeding, the message delivered, austerely back to his station beside the magnificent palm.

All this, because of my status as the great-nephew of an old Bukra whom he remembered with love and reverence, and because he discovered that I knew about tree-men and many other matters usually sealed books to Bukras, the old fellow who was the village patriarch, who, by right of his seniority, received and passed on from Silvio the messages from Silvio's brother the tree, amply substantiated.

There was nothing secretive about him, once he knew my interest in these things. Such procedure as securing the possession of a tree-man for his tribe seemed to the old man entirely reasonable; there was no necessary secret about it, certainly not from sympathetic me, the "yoong marster" of

Great Fountain Estate.

And Hans Grumbach, once he had finished with his roadwork, not being aware of all this, but sensing something out of the ordinary and hence to be feared about Silvio Fabricius and his palm tree, decided to end the stupidness out there. Grumbach decided to cut down the tree.

If I had had any inkling of this intention I could have saved Grumbach. It would have been a comparatively simple matter for me to have said enough to Carrington to have him forbid it; or, indeed, as a partner in the control of the estate, to forbid it myself. But I knew nothing about it, and have in my statement of his intention to destroy the tree supplied my own conception of his motives.

Grumbach, although virtually Caucasian in appearance, was of mixed blood, and quite without the Caucasian background of superior quality which makes the educated West Indian *mestizo* the splendid citizen he is in so many notable instances. His white ancestry was derived from a grandfather, a Schleswig-Holsteiner, who had been a sergeant of the Danish troops stationed on Santa Cruz and who, after the term of his enlistment had expired, had married into a respectable coloured family, and remained on the island. Grumbach was without the Caucasian aristocrat's tolerance for the preoccupations of the blacks. To him such affairs were "stupidness," merely. Like others of his kind he held the black people in a kind of contempt; was wholly, I imagine, without sympathy for them, though a worthy fellow enough in his limited way. And, perhaps, he had not enough Negro in him to understand instinctively even so much as what Silvio Fabricius, the tree-man, stood for in his community.

I had, too, you will remember, known something in those six years, of his view-points, his reactions to the "stupidness," and, specifically, some knowledge at least of his direct reaction, his pique and resentment, as these arose from his contacts with the tree-man. As I have indicated, the element of fear coloured this attitude.

He chose, cannily, one of the periods when Fabricius was away from his tree, reporting to the village. It was early in the afternoon, and Grumbach, having finished his road-work several days before, was directing a group of labourers who were grubbing ancient "bush"—heavy under-growth, brush, rank weeds, small trees—from along the winding trail which led from the village to the fountain or waterfall. This was now feeding a tumbling stream which Carrington intended to dam, lower down, for a central reserve reservoir.

The majority, if not all, of these labour-ers under his eye at the moment were new to the village; members of the increasing group which were coming into the restored stone cabins as fast as these became habit-able. They were cutting out the brush with machetes, canebills, and knives; and, for the small trees, a couple of axes were being used from time to time. This work was being done quite near the great tree, and from his position in the roadway overlook-ing his gang, Grumbach must have seen the tree-man leave his station and start towards the village with one of his "messages."

This opportunity—he had, unquestion-ably, made up his mind about it all—was too good to be lost. As I learned from the two men whom he detached from his grubbing-gang and took with him, Silvio Fabricius was hardly out of sight over the sweep of the lower portion of the great field near the upper edge of which the coconut-palm towered, when Grumbach called to the two axe-men to follow him, and, with a word to the rest of the gang, led the way across the field's edge to the tree.

About this time Carrington and I were returning from one of our inspections of the fountain. We had been up there several times of late, since the scheme for the dam had been working in our minds. We were returning towards the village and the construction work progressing there along that same pathway through the big field from which, years before, I had had my first sight of the tree-man.

As we came in sight of the tree, towards which I invariably looked when I was near it, I saw, of course, that Fabricius was not there. Grumbach and his two labourers stood under it, Grumbach talking to the men. One of them as we approached—we were still perhaps a hundred yards distant—shook his head emphatically. He told me later that Grumbach had led them straight to the tree and commanded them to chop it down.

Both men had demurred. They were not of the village, it is true, not, certainly, Dahomeyans. But—they had some idea, even after generations away from "Guinea," that here was something strange; something over which the suitable course was to "go stupid." Both men, therefore, "went stupid" forthwith.

Grumbach, as was usual with him, poor fellow, was vastly annoyed by this process. I could hear him barge out at the labourers; see him gesticulate. Then from the nearest, he seized the axe and attacked the tree himself. He struck a savage blow at it, then, gathering himself together, for he was stout like the middle-aged of all his class, and unused to such work, he struck again, somewhat above the place where the first axe-blow had landed on the tree.

"You'd better stop him, Carrington," said I, "and I will explain my reasons to you afterwards."

Carrington cupped his hands and shouted, and both negroes looked towards us. But Grumbach, apparently, had not heard, or, if he had, supposed that the words were directed to somebody other than himself. Thus, everybody within view was occupied, you will note—Carrington looking at Grumbach; the two labourers looking towards us; Grumbach intent upon making an impression on the tough coconut wood. I alone, for some instinctive reason, thought suddenly of Silvio Fabricius, and directed my gaze towards the point, down the long field, over which horizon he would appear when returning.

Perhaps it was the sound of the axe's impact against his brother the tree apprehended by a set of senses for seventeen years attuned to the tree's moods and rustlings, to the "messages" which his brother the tree imparted to him; perhaps some uncanny instinct merely, that arrested him in his course towards the village down there, carrying the current "message" from the tree about tomorrow's weather.

As I looked, Silvio Fabricius, running lightly, erect, came over the distant horizon of the lower field's bosomed slope. He stopped there, a distant figure, but clearly within my view. Without taking my eyes off him I spoke again to Carrington:

"You must stop Grumbach, Carrington—there's more in this than you know. Stop him—at once!"

And, as Carrington shouted a second time, Grumbach raised the axe for the third blow at the tree, the blow which did not land.

As the axe came up, Silvio Fabricius, a distant figure down there, reached for the small sharp canebill which hung beside him from his trouser-belt, a cutting tool with which he smoothed the bark of his brother the tree on occasion, cut out annually the choking mass of "cloth" from its top, removed fading fronds as soon as their decay reached the stage where they were no longer benefiting the tree, cut his coconuts. I could see the hot sunlight flash against the wide blade of the canebill as though it had been a small heliograph-mirror. Fabricius was about a thousand yards away. He raised the canebill empty in the air, and with it made a sudden, cutting, pulling motion downwards; a grave, almost a symbolic movement. Fascinated, I watched him return the canebill to its place, on its hook, fastened to the belt at the left side.

But, abruptly, my attention was distracted to what was going on nearer at hand. Carrington's shout died, half-uttered. Simultaneously I heard the yells of uncontrollable, sudden terror from the two labourers at the tree's foot. My eyes, snatched away from the distant tree-man, turned to

Carrington beside me, glimpsing a look of terrified apprehension; then, with the speed of thought, towards the tree where one labourer was in the act of falling face-downward on the ground—I caught the terrified white gleam of his rolled eyes—the other, twisting himself away from the tree towards us, the very personification of crude horror, his hands over his eyes. And my glance was turned just in time to see the great coconut which, detached from its heavy, fibrous cordage up there, sixty feet above the ground, struck Grumbach full and true on the wide pitch helmet which he affected, planterwise, against the sun.

He seemed almost to be driven into the ground by the impact. The axe flew off at an angle past the tree.

He never moved. And when, with the help of the two labourers, Carrington and I, having summoned a cart from the nearby road-gang cutting bushes, lifted the body, the head which had been that poor devil Grumbach's, was merely a mass of sodden pulp.

We took the body down the road in the cart, towards his newly erected manager's house. And a few yards along our way Silvio Fabricius passed us, running erectly, his sombre face expressionless, his stride a kind of dignified lope, glancing not to right or left, speeding straight to his brother the tree which had been injured in his absence.

Looking back, where the road took a turn, I saw him, leaning now close beside the tree, his long fingers probing the two gashes which Hans Grumbach, who would never swing another axe, had made there, about two feet above the ground; while aloft the glorious fronds of the massive tree burgeoned like great sails in the afternoon Trade.

Later that afternoon we sent the mortal remains of Hans Grumbach down the long hill road to Frederiksted in a cart, decently disposed, after telephoning his wife's relatives to break the sorrowful news to her. It was Carrington who telephoned, at my suggestion. I told him that they would appreciate it, he being the head of the company. Such *nuances* have their meaning in the West Indies where the finer shades are of an importance. He explained that it was an accident, gave the particulars as he had seen them with his own eyes—Grumbach had been working under a tall coconut-palm and a heavy coconut, falling, had struck him and killed him instantly. It had been a quite merciful death.

The next morning I walked up towards the fountain again, alone, after a sleepless night of cogitation. I walked across the section of field between the newly-grubbed roadside and the great tree. I walked straight up to the tree-man, stood beside him. He paid no attention to me whatever. I spoke to him:

"Fabricius," said I, "it is necessary that I should speak to you."

The tree-man turned his gaze upon me gravely. Seen thus, face to face, he was a remarkably handsome fellow, now about thirty years of age, his features regular, his expression calm, inscrutable; wise with a wisdom certainly not Caucasian, such as to put into my mind the phrase: "not of this world." He bowed, gravely, as though assuring me of his attention.

I said: "I was looking at you yesterday

afternoon when you came back to your tree, over the lower end of the field —down there." I indicated where he had stood with a gesture. Again he bowed, without any change of expression.

"I wish to have you know," I continued, "that I understand; that no one else besides me saw you, saw what you did—with the canebill, I mean. I wish you to know that what I saw I am keeping to myself. That is all."

Silvio Fabricius the tree-man continued to look into my face, without any visible change whatever in his expression. For the third time he nodded, presumably to indicate that he understood what I had said, but utterly without any emotion whatever. Then, in a deep, resonant voice, he spoke to me, the first and last time I have ever heard him utter a word.

"Yo' loike to know, yoong marster," said he, with an im-pressive gravity, "me brudda,"—he placed a hand against the tree's smooth trunk—"t'ink hoighly 'bout yo', sar. Ahlso 'bout de enterprise fo pineopples. Him please', sar, yoong marster; him indicate-me yo' course be serene an' ahlso of a profit." The tree-man bowed again, and without another word or so much as a glance in my direction, detaching his attention from me as deliberately as he had given it when I first spoke to him, he turned towards his brother the tree, laid his face against its bark, and slowly encircled the massive trunk with his two great muscular black arms.

I arrived on the island in the middle of October, 1928, coming down as usual from New York after my summer in the States. Great Fountain had suffered severely in the hurricane of the previous month, and when I arrived there I found Carrington well along with the processes of restoration. Many precautions had been taken beforehand and our property had been damaged because of these much less than the other estates. I had told Carrington, who had a certain respect for my familiarity with "native manners

(Continued on page 119)

Henry St. Clair Whitehead (1882–1932) was an Episcopal minister and author of horror and fantasy fiction. He died in 1932, but new works of his fiction were discovered and publishing sporadically over the years.

"Tree-Man" stars Whitehead's occult detective Gerald Canevin, who frequently investigated cases with voodoo overtones. Canevin appeared in 16 stories, frequently in *Weird Tales*. "The Trap," published in *Strange Tales of Mystery and Terror* (March 1932), was written in collaboration with his friend H.P. Lovecraft.

Tree-Man

(Continued from page 118)

and customs," enough about the tree-man and his functions tribally to cause him to heed the warning, transmitted by the now nearly helpless old patriarch of the village, and brought in by the tree-man four days before the hurricane broke—and two days before the government cable-advice had reached the island.

Silvio Fabricius had stayed beside his tree. On the third day, when it was for the first time possible for the villagers to get as far as the upper end of the great field near the fountain, he had been found, Carrington reported to me, lying in the field, dead, his face composed inscrutably, the great trunk of his brother the tree across his chest which had been crushed by its great weight when it had been uprooted by the wind and fallen.

And until they wore off there had been smears of earth, Carrington said, on the heads and faces of all the original Dahomeyan villagers and upon the heads and faces of several of the newer labourer families as well. ∎

Dateline: 1920

The Mark of Zorro opens in theaters nationwide December 5, 1920. Zorro made his world debut in *The All-Story Weekly* magazine (dated August 9, 1919) in *The Curse of Capistrano* by Johnston McCulley's. The film receives praise from critics and audiences alike. Screen idol Douglas Fairbanks, Sr. is priased for his performances as Don Diego de la Vega and his masked persona.

ABRAHAM STROUD

Inventor, scientist, CEO,
Vampire hunter ...

He knew the job was dangerous ...

BLOODSCREAMS™

by ROBERT W. WALKER

A cross between Nikola Tesla and T.E. Lawrence; a direct descendant of Abraham Van Helsing, maintaining the family business — hunting vampires and supernatural vermin. Follow along if you dare ...

Werewoman
(Continued from page 104)

sweet, life-giving air that humanity breathes swept in a flood across the barrens, blowing away all the shadowy, unclean creatures to whom it had been haven for so long. He knew — *he knew* …

Greyness swooped round him, and all knowledge faded from his mind and the wind roared mightily in his ears. Somewhere in that roaring flight oblivion overtook him.

When he opened his eyes again he could not for an instant imagine where hc lay or what had happened. Weight pressed upon his entire body suffocatingly, pain shot through it in jagged flashes. His shoulder ached deeply. And the night was dark, dark about him. Something muffling and heavy had closed over his senses, for no longer could he hear the tiny, sharp sounds of the plain or scent those tingling odors that once blew along the wind. Even the chattering overhead had fallen still. The place did not even smell the same. He thought he could catch from afar the odor of smoke, and somehow the air, as nearly as he could tell with his deadened senses, no longer breathed of desolation and loneliness. The smell of life was in the wind, very faintly. Little pleasant odors of flower-scent and kitchen smoke seemed to tinge it.

"—wolves must have gone," someone was saying above him. "They stopped howling a few minutes ago—notice?—first time since we came into this damned place. Listen."

With a painful effort Smith rolled his head sideways and stared. A little group of men was gathered around him, their eyes lifted just now to the dark horizon. In the new density of the night he could not see them clearly, and he blinked in irritation, striving to regain that old, keen, clarity he had lost. But they looked familiar. One wore a white fur cap on his head. Someone said, indicating something beyond Smith's limited range of vision, "Fellow here must have had quite a tussle. See the dead she-wolf with her throat torn out? And look—all the wolf-tracks everywhere in the dust. Hundreds of them. I wonder ..."

"Bad luck to talk about them," broke in the fur-capped leader. "Werewolves, I tell you—I've been in this place before, and I know. But I never saw or heard tell of a thing like what we saw tonight—that big white-eyed one running with the she-wolves. God! I'll never forget those eyes."

Smith moved his head and groaned. The men turned quickly. "Look, he's coming to," said someone, and Smith was vaguely conscious of an arm under his head and some liquid, hot and strong, forced between his lips. He opened his eyes and looked up. The fur-capped man was bending over him. Their eyes met. In the starlight, Smith's were colorless as pale steel.

The man choked something inarticulate and leaped back so suddenly that the flask spilled its contents half over Smith's chest. He crossed himself frankly with a hand that shook.

"Who—who are you?" he demanded unsteadily.

Smith grinned wearily and closed his eyes. ∎

Case Gray

(Continued from page 38)

"So one got away?" Rita asked.

Winchester and Preston looked at each other warily.

"What?" Rita persisted.

Hawk looked squarely at Justice. "Rick. I'm pretty sure… pretty sure it was…"

"Go ahead, Hawk," Justice prompted.

"I think it was Marlene."

The only sound on the Gondola was the murmur of the engines and the whoosh of the wind.

Rita Marshall's face hardened, her fine features chiseled. "That bitch is alive?"

"I could be wrong, Rick," Winchester offered. "I only caught a quick glimpse."

"Hawk," Preston interjected. "She smiled at us. She waved as she took off."

Justice was silent for a moment. His features remained impassive. When he spoke, his voice was strangely distant.

"I don't think there is much doubt we should prepare ourselves for trouble." All eyes were on him. "The Scarlet Harlot has returned." ∎

Bloody Bill Obeys

(Continued from page 48)

the steep bank to the river, and peeled off his clothes.

Then, without warning, but with every indication of extreme urgency in its tones the voice countermanded its instructions.

"No, no, don't take them all off. Never mind. That's enough. Wake up. Come out of it. Snap awake!"

Dimly Bill became aware of a huge glare of lights. Faintly he could hear a roar which sounded like the clapping of hands, mingled with peals of laughter. Shaking off a momentary stupor he suddenly found himself, shirt off, trousers partially unbut-

toned, shoes removed, toes gleaming through holes in his socks, standing before the footlights of the Colma Opera House.

Before him, smiling, serene, confident, stood Morton the Mystic. Behind the footlights the house thundered its applause, roared its laughter.

On the stage a toy automobile, such as children pedal around the streets in, lay on its side, a rubber knife, painted to look like steel, sat on the table beside a stuffed dummy.

Slowly Bill's light-dazzled eyes took in these things. Then he spat on the stage.

"Aw shucks!" he said. ∎

Next Issue:

Another lost story by Erle Stanley Gardner, newly rediscovered; 'The Nymph in the Keyhole,' hardboiled thriller by Charles Boeckman; classic SF by E.C. Tubb; New Pulp Fiction, another 'Retro Review,' and scholarly pieces.

Pulp Adventures #37 — Fall 2020 issue on sale October 31st!

High Sea Adventure
by Steven L. Rowe

The Brotherhood of the Black Flag resorted to piracy to live free — None of them suspected the price freedom would demand.

Sea Road to Neverland & **Hook of the Jolly Roger** — Two rollicking prequels to Peter Pan! How *did* 'Captain Hook' get his *nom de guerre* with two perfectly good hands?

https://www.facebook.com/Steven.L.Rowe.102

Amethyst Eyes
(Continued from page 74)

crimson staining his beard, those words unsaid.

Instead, Ranulfr forced his legs to move, to make a step towards her. She watched his efforts and the smile grew on her face as she understood. All trace of worry vanished as she watched his bleeding, failing form stagger a pace and then a second one.

Three paces Ranulfr made, and no more. Exhaustion, loss of blood, the damage done by his many wounds, all conspired to bring him down. He fell, his sight blurred, darkened, was lost entircly. Unseen by him, those amethyst eyes and cool red lips showed admiration as well as joy.

When Ranulfr stood again, he had only eyes for the vision before him. Pain and weakness were a fading memory. The battle he had won was of no consequence. He did not bother to seek weapons or search the surrounding forest for more enemies. Such matters would concern him no longer. Only the woman before him mattered.

Her calm reserve was broken. Shield back on her arm, spear held in shield hand, she reached out her free hand to Ranulfr, the invitation clear without words. Behind her, the horse came forward, eager for the long ride home. The rainbow bridge was far off and shining Valhalla further still.

Paying no heed to the bloody, butchered carcasses around him, not even to his own, Ranulfr stepped forward to take the hand of the Valkyrie with the welcoming amethyst eyes.   ∎

Mona's Back

(Continued from page 67)

I looked to Mona, perplexed, and then back to the grinning, pompous face of Darius Edwards. He walked in, sidled right up close to Mona and kissed her on the lips.

"Like I said," Mona laughed through a smile pulled straight and hard, eyes firing with a gleam to give the devil a run for his money. "A man never knows when a woman is lying."

My mouth was open and Edwards was chucking words down my throat.

"When they read the Leech's will you and everyone else in this town will find he left everything to his grandson with his mother as custodian. I should know; I framed it. There will also be a confession found in his safe, from Jimmy Bones, recounting his murdering Artie Levin and stealing those gems, framing poor Mona. What could she do but run to protect her child?"

The lawyer threw an arm around Mona's shoulder. She just melted into place like wax around a candlewick.

"With Brasno and Jimmy dead," Edwards went on smoothly, his manner dark and nasty, "and the disks oddly having disappeared from the evidence room, it's our organization, our town now."

"I told Darius you'd fix it for us Jack."

I just stood there, the stupid gingerbread boy riding on the fox's nose. At once Mona disengaged herself and slid to the still open backdoor.

"Now get out!" she growled. "And when you see the old gang and they ask what happened, you tell them, Jack; you tell them. You tell them all, Mona's back!" ■

A Leather Soul, Maybe

by E. DOYLE GILLESPIE

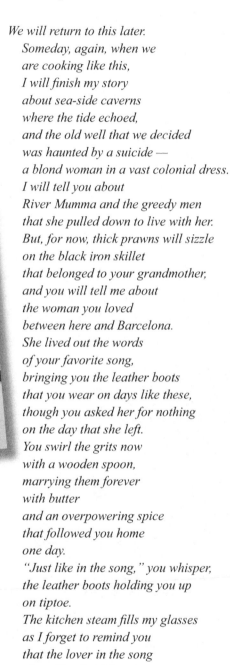

We will return to this later.
Someday, again, when we
are cooking like this,
I will finish my story
about sea-side caverns
where the tide echoed,
and the old well that we decided
was haunted by a suicide —
a blond woman in a vast colonial dress.
I will tell you about
River Mumma and the greedy men
that she pulled down to live with her.
But, for now, thick prawns will sizzle
on the black iron skillet
that belonged to your grandmother,
and you will tell me about
the woman you loved
between here and Barcelona.
She lived out the words
of your favorite song,
bringing you the leather boots
that you wear on days like these,
though you asked her for nothing
on the day that she left.
You swirl the grits now
with a wooden spoon,
marrying them forever
with butter
and an overpowering spice
that followed you home
one day.
"Just like in the song," you whisper,
the leather boots holding you up
on tiptoe.
The kitchen steam fills my glasses
as I forget to remind you
that the lover in the song
also offered gold,
also offered silver,
and, when Bob Dylan struck the last chord,
had still not returned from the sea.

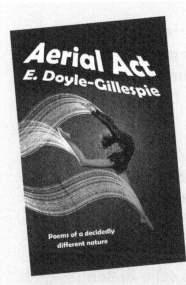

Edward Doyle-Gillespie, a Baltimore policeman, is the author of *Aerial Act: Poems of a Decidedly Different Nature* (Bold Venture Press, 2020). In the volume, he shares a sampling of the human condition, shows how life consumes itself to live again, and exhibits a body enduring trauma reborn to find a new voice. The author describes spirits abandoning the flesh to create mythology, and even sex intertwining with the taint of death. He is the author of *Masala Tea and Oranges, On the Later Addition of Sancho Panza,* and *Socorro Prophesy.*

AERIAL ACT by E. Doyle Gillespie
www.boldventurepress.com

JOIN THE PULP SAFARI!

Every issue is a quarterly safari through the Pulp Jungle genres — western, mystery, romance, humor, weird terror, science fiction, and super-heroes!

Classic pulp fiction, new pulp fiction, articles about pulp magazines and the people who made them great!

Past issues have featured Zorro; the Cisco Kid; Dan Turner, Hollywood Detective ... Robert Leslie Bellem, Johnston McCulley, O. Henry, Walt Coburn, Judson P. Philips, E. Hoffmann Price, Arthur J. Burks, Gardner F. Fox, G.T. Fleming Roberts, and many more!

Check our website for descriptions of each issue's contents.

www.boldventurepress.com

KILLER'S CHOICE

By EARLE BASINSKY

THE FOG COVERED everything, blanketing the earth in a thick billow of murky white. Far out in the harbor a horn brayed, echoing hollowly across the water and rolling in toward the river docks. The little boats swung and lifted gently in the water, grating easily with a soft rasping noise as they bumped the slime encrusted pilings.

Alan whistled tunelessly as he walked through the fog along the dock. Maybe he could get out in it tonight, but he doubted it. The fog was too thick, and there was no wind. Not much chance of it dissipating before morning.

As he neared the spot where his little gasoline boat lay moored, a shapeless figure moved toward him noiselessly through the heavy whiteness. Alan stopped sharply, not daring to move as he felt a gun thrust tightly against his stomach!

A gruff voice said: "Okay, hold it! Don't move!"

Originally Published In
Vic Verity Magazine #4
Don Fortune Publishing Company
(Cover art: C.C. Beck)

For a moment, all was silence. Then, "You own one of these boats?"

"Yes," Allan replied, making an effort to keep his voice steady.

"Then I gotta job for you. Will you take it?" The gun trembled against Alan.

"I don't know. It depends. I never had a guy stick a gun in my stomach before …"

"I gotta get across this river. I can't swim. So you've gotta take me!" His voice rose sharply, and Alan felt the gun tremble again, ever so slightly.

"Take it easy," Alan said. "Sure, I'll take you. Sure. What's in it for me?"

"A hundred bucks … and your life! Because if you don't…!"

"I said I'd take you. But this fog is nasty. It might be dangerous. I don't know if we can make it in this low tide."

"What difference does that make? I gotta get across! I can't go no further on this side. Once I'm across, I can …" His voice had a desperate, pleading whine to it.

Then Alan said, "Put that gun away. I'll take you. But we've got to get in my boat first. It's over here."

The gun moved from Alan's stomach. But the figure was still tense. "Okay, but no funny business. I still got my hand close to the trigger!"

"Mind if I light a cigarette?" Alan asked, as they walked along.

"Naw, just remember what I said. One false move, Mac, and …"

Alan lighted his cigarette. The yellow light from the match flared up and for a moment he caught a glimpse of the man's face who was walking by his side. A hawk nose, flanked by narrow bloodshot eyes, peered from under a shapeless hat. Alan stiffened, letting out an involuntary gasp of surprise.

The man chuckled grimly. "All right so you know who I am. That oughta convince you I ain't kiddin'. But I got nothin' to lose either way. One more killin' ain't gonna make no difference. Understand?"

"Yes." Alan gulped nervously. He had seen the guy's picture in the paper for the last three days. His name was "Rocky" Graham. Every cop in the country was looking for him. "Shoot-to-kill" was Rocky's philosophy in a nutshell.

Now they had reached the boat. "Get

in," Alan said.

"Rocky" got in, but he turned and faced Alan so he could see every move he made. Then Alan knelt down by the motor and wound the rope around the flywheel. Adjusting the spark, he pulled sharply on the rope and the motor kicked softly into life. The little boat throbbed under them as Alan untied the mooring rope and they eased away from the dock.

"Rocky" sat down on a little seat facing Alan. The fog closed in on them, and the docks disappeared from sight when they had gone less than five feet. Alan leaned back against his seat. His hand rested against the bottom of the boat. A few inches away there was a heavy steel wrench. He inched his hand behind him, hoping "Rocky" wouldn't notice the movement. Then his fingers touched the wrench, and he began to drag it toward him. He was all set to lift his arm and hurl it at "Rocky's" head …

"Okay, I seen ya! Drop it!" "Rocky's" voice was ugly from the front of the boat.

ALAN SIGHED and tossed the wrench overboard. It disappeared in the fog and hit with a dull splash. That was that.

"Now, no more funny stuff, see!"

"You win," Alan murmured.

They moved smoothly along, and Alan started thinking. This guy is a killer … I've got to do something … I can't just sit here and let this happen to me … Maybe I could …

He knew the river almost as well as the palm of his own hand, while "Rocky" knew nothing. "Rocky" was depending on him entirely to get him to the other side of the river, but in the fog, he couldn't tell where

they were going … and the tide was *low*.

Gently Alan turned the wheel slightly to the right. He could feel the nose of the boat swinging to the left, but he knew "Rocky," unused to riding on water, couldn't feel it. And for the next half hour the boat swung in a large circle. The fog made everything seem unreal, ghostlike.

"Rocky" sat motionless, watching him. Then, "How much longer?"

"About half an hour," Alan replied calmly.

He breathed a silent prayer. He hoped his calculations were correct. But in this dense fog he couldn't be sure of anything. As the boat circled, they drifted with the tide …

"Better not make any more slip ups," "Rocky" growled. Alan did not answer.

AS TIME PASSED, Alan began to worry. This blasted fog! How could he be sure of what he was doing? Suddenly the boat grated on sandy bottom! He felt a flood of relief rush over him. "Rocky" stood up in the front of the boat.

"This is it." Alan said. "How about my hundred bucks?"

"You'll take fifty and like it!" "Rocky" snarled. "The job wasn't worth that much dough anyway!" He handed Alan a few bills, and stepped over the side of the boat into knee deep water.

"Rocky" waded toward higher ground, and Alan blasted on full throttle. The boat streaked off into the fog. He made a sharp turn to the right and then cut the motor so "Rocky" couldn't locate his position by sound.

From where he was, Alan could hear

every move "Rocky" made. He heard splashing and then a curse. "What th—! Water on both sides! The dirty louse!"

Alan called calmly from the silent, drifting boat. "Yeah, you're on a sand bar in the middle of the river, killer!"

B LAM! BLAM! "Rocky's" gun roared twice, cutting through the fog. After that, all that was heard was the sounds made by the lapping waves on the sand. "Rocky" was listening, waiting for Alan to make a move.

"You don't know where I am, killer. Better save your bullets. It'll be high tide in a few hours and the water will be over your head. It was nice of you to tell me you couldn't swim … remember?"

Alan started the motor again, and "Rocky's" gun boomed out.

"Better save at least one bullet. It's better than drowning or being picked up by the cops! So long, killer! Take your choice!"   ∎

Earle Basinsky (1921-1963), sometimes credited as "Jr.," attended law school in 1939 but left in 1942 to join the U.S. Air Force. While stationed in Greenwood, he met and befriended Mickey Spillane.

He married in 1945 and moved to Brooklyn, where he worked with Spillane. He had some success selling fiction, but began working in his father's print shop upon returning to Vicksburg. Years later, a chance encounter with Spillane encouraged him to return to writing.

Basinsky published three short stories in crime-fiction magazines, three text stories in comic books, and two full-length novels. Critical assessment of his work ranged from positive to dismissive.

Made in the USA
Monee, IL
13 June 2021